GOLK

GOLK

GOLK

GOLK

GOLK

GOLK

GOLK

GOLK

Other Phoenix Fiction titles from Chicago

RICHARD G. STERN

GOLK

With a new Foreword by
BERNARD F. RODGERS, JR.

THE UNIVERSITY OF CHICAGO PRESS
Chicago & London

The University of Chicago Press, Chicago 60637
The University of Chicago Press, Ltd., London

96 95 94 93 92 91 90 89 88 87   5 4 3 2 1

Library of Congress Cataloging in Publication Data

Stern, Richard G., 1928–
    Golk.

    (Phoenix fiction)
    Reprint. Originally published: New York :
Criterion Books, 1960.   I. Title.   II. Series.
PS3569.T39G6   1987   813'.54   87–16217
ISBN 0–226–77319–1 (pbk.)

H. G. S.
and
M. V. S.
with
love

FOREWORD

Bernard Rodgers

WHEN the American Academy and Institute of Arts and Letters selected Richard Stern as the recipient of its Medal of Merit in February 1985, most of the body of work for which he was being honored was out of print. With this Phoenix Fiction reprint of *Golk*, the majority of his novels—including *In Any Case* (reissued as *The Chaleur Network*), *Stitch*, *Other Men's Daughters*, *Natural Shocks*, and *A Father's Words*—are once again available both to those who have admired his work for years and to those who are just discovering it.

An how much there is to admire and discover.

"Novelists count only as they are distinct from other novelists," Stern once wrote. "Everything that is different about them becomes their stock in trade." The republication of *Golk* invites us to consider what the distinctive character of Richard Stern's own fiction has been; and rereading *Golk* in relation to the other novels currently in print makes that character clear.

Golk is a first novel, and it shows. While it introduces a narrative voice that will shortly become recognizable, that voice is not yet fully under control; while it sketches what will become Stern's recurrent themes, conflicts, and character types, these have not yet been given their mature forms. So in *Golk* we can see Stern struggling to create a voice that will allow him to mix the street and the library, what he has seen and heard and what he has read and thought. That distinctive narrative voice is already largely here and largely successful. But the struggle is apparent in the novel's few false notes—in what now appears offensive in the treatment of the black woman, Elaine, and artificial in the love scenes of Hondorp and Hendricks. (By his third novel, *The Chaleur Network*, such false notes will have disappeared entirely.)

What will emerge as the persistent concerns of Stern's mature fiction—the challenges of change, the burdens of moral responsibility, the nature of fatherhood and the emotional entanglements of the domestic life, a fascination with power—are also already evident. But in *Golk* these concerns are uncharacteristically combined with a wildly comic satire of television. And the satire is so good that it all but overwhelms Stern's focus on the Hondorps and Golk.

In *Golk*, these characteristic concerns and this satire are interwoven from the novel's opening pages, where Stern's first hero Hondorp, an unemployed observer of life and pampered son, is suddenly drawn into the world of the popular television program "You're On Camera" and its creator, Golk. But the wit and insight of Stern's treatment of what was then the relatively new medium of television often makes Hondorp's conversion from an observer of life into participant seem secondary. In fact, twenty-seven years after its initial publication, *Golk* remains noteworthy as one of the first—and, with Kosinski's *Being There*, still one of the few—treatments of the character and impact of television in serious American fiction. Its moving and hilarious portrait of Poppa Hondorp, mesmerized in front of the screen; its black comic treatment of the world of ratings battles, midlevel media managers, and godlike network moguls that would later be captured in the film *Network;* its witty demonstration of how this powerful new medium quickly began to create its own language; its exploration of Golk's and Hondorp's Faustian bargains with the medium—all retain their freshness.

Although the satire of television dominates this first novel, *Golk* is also an introduction to the concerns of the books that will follow it. In its fascination with power—the power of television, of Golk and, on an infinitely higher level, of Parisak, the empire builder who sits atop the midtown skyscraper that bears his name in an office hermetically sealed and fully and magically automated—it touches on a subject that will continue to intrigue Stern throughout his career.

In Hondorp's story we can also detect Stern's first treatment of other themes that will emerge to dominate his subsequent fiction. All of Stern's novels focus on characters confronted with jarring changes—changes that disrupt their equilibrium and challenge their sense of themselves and their closest relationships. "Life surprised me," his Professor Merriweather will explain to the father of the young woman with whom he is having an affair in *Other Men's Daughters*. "Life still had surprises up its sleeve. (Sometimes it seemed all sleeve)," Cy Riemer will echo in *A Father's Words*. And what will be true for these later heroes is also true for Hondorp, from the moment that Golk finds him browsing in a bookshop until the novel's final pages.

In Hondorp's case, life's surprise is an unexpected chance to be somebody and do something after years of floating aimlessly. For him, as for the later heroes, that surprise quickly turns into a moral challenge. How far will Hondorp be willing to go in pursuit of the main chance? How will he respond when his newly-discovered desires and ambitions come to conflict with what he owes to his father and to Golk?

As Fred Wursup will put the recurrent question in *Natural Shocks*, "How much of life do you owe to another person?" "If you're a father, a husband, a son, a lover, a worker, how divide yourself, your sympathy, energy, time, money? Is the act of division itself treason?" "How much was one supposed to do?" Cy Riemer will ask as he lets his son walk away from him on a Manhattan street. "Sometimes," he thinks in words that express what all Stern's heroes feel at one time or another, "I feel I'm nothing but my bonds."

In Stern's fiction, the most important bonds are always those of fatherhood. Where Philip Roth's heroes are, above all, sons, where Saul Bellow's are, above all, ex-husbands, Stern's are most often and most importantly fathers. Like John Updike's or John Irving's, his novels are full of a parent's heartrending doubts and fears, a father's sometimes inarticulate but always profound feelings toward his children. And if *Golk* is atypical in that it focuses on a son's emotions rather than a father's, the book's father, Poppa Hondorp, and its other father figure, Golk, light up every page on which they appear in a way that often leaves Hondorp himself in the narrative's shadows.

The father-son relationship, Poppa Hondorp explains as he himself is being golked (by Golk), is "noble"—but "packed to the margins, packed, impacted, with heartbreak. . . . The matter is not treason, just—how shall I say it?—a carelessness, inattention, lack of thought, but terrible, all terrible. Worse might be better. You would be stiffened to resist. But against so soft a thing, who can push?" And he goes on to compare a father's heart to an hourglass, in which filial love runs out "the thin neck of old age."

Poppa Hondorp is a classic of fatherhood: an unforgettable combination of warmth and self-pity, of affection and need, of possessiveness and manipulation. Although none of Stern's later fathers will be quite as funny, all will share his emotional attachments. "I was a terrible father to my son, at least until it was too late for him to know otherwise," *The Chaleur Network* begins. (If Hondorp had had more self-awareness, *Golk* might have *ended* with the opening clause reversed.) "For me, family counted," Riemer explains in *A Father's Words*. "Though I was not much of a son (and perhaps not much of a father). . . ." *The Chaleur Network* traces a father's odyssey across postwar Europe in an effort to vindicate his dead son's reputation; in *Stitch*, Edward Gunther carries his twenty-two month-old son across a Venetian square, "kissing him on the cheeks and under the ear, muttering his name. This," he thinks, is "what counted." Merriweather describes holding his young son in bed as a purer moment of love than any other he has ever known; after his separation from them, Wursup climbs to the roof of his building to watch his children move about the apartment across the street. And Riemer, Stern's masterpiece of fatherhood, sets off on a cross-country plane trip to see and try to make peace with each of his children.

But the fatherhood of Stern's heroes is complicated, as Poppa Hondorp's relationship to his son is, by their own egos and desires. Like Edward Gunther, each is faced with the question of why he "couldn't lose himself in what counted, what belonged to him, what was his human duty to assist and care for." Each, like Hondorp, finds himself struggling to accept his responsibility to those he loves. Each, like Gunther, seems stymied by the sense that "first he has to understand what he was" and realizes that "a rusty, backfiring, clotted ego" will not serve; that he must "clean out the heart." The cleansing is never easy, and Stern's novels are a record of its complications.

These complications may be traced, in part, to the fact that Hondorp and Stern's subsequent heroes are, like Gunther, "an unstable mixture of sensitivity and opacity"; that, like Wursup, each struggles with a sense that there are "glacial rifts" in him, "times when he was as unfeeling as the chemicals which made him." And each, like Gunther, must struggle with "the irreconcilability of his attachments." They are not just fathers, after all, but fathers met in the midst of or just after the breakup of marriages, about to be or just recently separated from their children. More often than not, they are already involved with yet unable to commit themselves fully to another woman. And after his fathers and their children, the most important characters in Stern's novels are these women and the ex-wives. Hendricks is a first version of the type: attractive, talented, strong-minded, yet somehow thwarted. Her sisters in the later novels will also be insecure and unbalanced by their lovers' or husbands' self-involvement. The dissolution of Hondorp's marriage, his failure to establish a relationship that he can fully commit himself to, sets the pattern for the many estrangements that will follow.

The familial struggles, paternal feelings, and moral quandaries of Stern's novels take on their distinctive character because of the particular nature of his settings—cities like New York, Chicago, Paris, Venice, Rome—and of his heroes. Urbane, witty, garrulous, highly educated, reflective, self-conscious, they allow him the broad range of cultural and contemporary allusion his own erudition requires. Herbert Hondorp the autodidact is succeeded by Gunther, the failed theoretical physicist and aspiring amateur man of letters; by Merriweather, the physiologist and Harvard professor; by Wursup, the globe-trotting nationally-known journalist; and by Riemer, the author and editor of a highly-respected newsletter. And their thoughts and observations, their voices, are the foundations upon which Stern's novels and their conflicts are built.

Like Bellow's heroes and Roth's, each of these men confronts the fact that familiarity with the world's culture does not make handling the mundane problems of the world's daily business of living and loving any easier. But because of their characters, their confrontations always turn out to be both engaging and revealing. Beginning with Hondorp, each grows, changes, learns. How they grow and change, what they learn, is what Stern's novels from *Golk* on are mainly about.

"To be decent," Wursup thinks. "Just to be decent." No small ambition, Stern keeps telling us; but what ambition matters more?

CHAPTER ONE

I

HONDORP passed the first part of his afternoon fingering ten-thousand-dollar carpets in the dim quarters of Surji-bulagh Fils, Teheran, Paris, London, and New York. 'Since I'd spent so many pleasant hours in your French and Persian shops,' he told the respectful clerk, 'I thought I'd give the Madison Avenue version the once-over before I committed myself elsewhere.'

The Persian knew that the Teheran branch was an inaccessible factory, but discounted Hondorp's claim as a curious and not displeasing form of American courtesy. He even inquired about Monsieur Tupkhaneh.

'The small dark man with the nice smile?' asked Hondorp.

The clerk smiled nicely himself and went on to the marvellous view of the city from Elburz. Hondorp had consulted the *Britannica* entry on Teheran before leaving home that morning but couldn't remember whether Elburz was a mountain, a fortress, or the river. In any case, he felt free to certify to the view's splendour, did so, and then asked whether the masterpiece at his feet was worked with the Sehna or the Ghiordes knot. The clerk's face split with bliss, and he launched into an account of the two great schools of carpet-weaving, hardly aware that he'd evaded a difficult query.

Hondorp had calculated that he could stay safely for an hour and a half, but the disquisition alone lasted forty minutes. For the next two hours, he sustained his interest in carpets and the clerk's confidence in the utility of his interest. Then, his practised eye caught that flicker of weariness which precedes suspicion. He felt a corresponding weariness himself and refused a fifth cup of coffee.

'I'll have to work this around in my mind for a couple of days,' he said, and let the thick intricacy drop from his hands into the clerk's devoted paws. 'Gulistan, Gulistan,' he muttered, and he was at the door nodding stiffly to the clerk's farewell effusion and descending the carpeted stairway to the street.

It was a handsome day, the first of the season on which people wore no top-coats. Hondorp balanced on the sill soaking in the warmth and gathering strength for his next visit. 'Books,' he thought. '*Eine Bücherei*.' He hadn't visited a bookstore for nearly a week. 'The unnourished mind withers,' was an old pronouncement of his father's, although the old man's reading had for years been confined to the *Journal of Ophthalmology* and *TV Guide*. He walked south for a block, turned east for two, and then, on Lexington, walked half a block farther south to Follett's, a store he hadn't been in for five or six months.

Hondorp usually didn't bother with window displays, but he stopped in front of Follett's to vent some spleen on the pyramid of Mlle Sagan's books which framed a picture of her uncertain, but distinctly come-on-buy-me smile. Hondorp's emotional life was composed largely of antipathies, and the most recent literary objects of his detestation were the bored young women of France and the angry young men of England. He regarded the bored Gioconda with contempt and fury, abstracted the factitious sadness from the rodent face, scalped from bangs to bun, felt himself dig out the slithering contents of the skull and trample them in the gutter; then, puffed with relief, he went in the store, quickly, purposively, past the tables of new books to the shabby alcoves whose shelves and tables held the secondhand books for which he had an affinity that he had never cared to analyse.

He'd just started picking his way through the history shelves, thumbing Motley on the Dutch Republic, when a voice, sharp with insolence, asked at his elbow, 'You looking or buying?'

The professional browser's ire rose in Hondorp, and he turned to grind the inquirer into dust. Dust there already was in the alcove, three solid walls of books, and five or six unusually bright, naked bulbs, but nothing else, nothing that could question his motives.

'Jesus,' growled Hondorp, and he rubbed his index finger against his right temple.

'What was that?' asked the voice. 'You'll have to tune up the volume a little. I'm in the wall here.'

Hondorp took off his reading glasses, wiped his eye sockets with a handkerchief, and studied the apparently inorganic wall.

'Here,' said the voice helpfully.

It seemed to be coming out of a Book League of America copy of *The Conquest of Peru*. Hondorp reached for the book, took it down, and put his face to the dark hole. 'Muuuuaaaaghh,' was his response to the four years' worth of dust which assaulted his nostrils.

He was jamming the book back in to plug the dike when the voice, with a kind of pleading authority, said, 'Read me a sentence or two.'

'Shove it,' was what Hondorp began to say, but a constraint learned from hours and hours of extricating himself from humiliations translated this into 'With pleasure.' He blew a small cloud of dust from the book, opened it and read:

Drawing his sword, he traced a line with it on the sand from east to west. Then, turning towards the south,

9

'Friends and comrades!' he said. 'On that side are toil, hunger, nakedness, the drenching storm, desertion, and death; on this side ease and pleasure. There lies Peru with its riches; here, Panama and its poverty. Choose, each man, what best becomes a brave Castillian. For my part, I go to the south!' So saying, he stepped across the line.

'So who is that "he"?' asked the voice, as if it had been personally insulted by the passage.

Hondorp turned back a page, saw that the 'he' was Pizarro, restrained himself from a phonemically related obscenity, held the book to the wall, and said, 'Take a look yourself.'

'Can't quite make it out,' said the voice after a few seconds. 'Print's too small.'

'All right,' said Hondorp wearily. 'What's the gag?'

'I missed that,' said the voice. 'Closer to the wall.' Hondorp moved closer. 'Now turn up the volume.' Hondorp repeated his question loudly.

'Guess,' said the voice.

'Some sort of smart-aleck promotion,' said Hondorp. 'Some stupid promotion gimmick, though what you think you can promote in this junk heap I don't know.'

As if it were a proper sequitur, the voice asked, 'Why do you like secondhand books?'

Hondorp, unconscious that the direction of inquiry had shifted, pondered and replied, 'They're cheaper, and they're not new.'

'What's the matter with new books? The whole economy runs along on people liking what's new. You stick with old books, and you're stringing up publishers, booksellers, authors, paper manufacturers, printers, linotypers, delivery boys, glue makers, and God knows who else. You like secondhand books and the economy stagnates.'

This speech took Hondorp into the familiar country of his contempt for the world's business, and his chin tilted up to the proper stance of this country, sufficient response to the belligerence from across the frontier.

But it proved insufficient for the voice, which pursued, 'What was that? I missed that.'

'I said nothing.'

'That won't do,' snapped the voice. 'Answer.'

'The economy,' answered Hondorp, surprised at his obedience, 'can drop dead for my money.'

'Ha, ha, ha. Not bad,' said the voice. 'Now tell me what your business is, pal?'

Every man has a question which terrifies him, and to the avoidance of which he gives himself with an energy that helps shape his life. This was the question that shoved Hondorp's diaphragm against his stomach, stiffened his throat muscles, hacked at his breath. Somehow, this time, he subdued the symptoms quickly. 'Whatever it is is none of yours, pal.'

At this, Hondorp heard a gasp, a gasp which didn't come from the wall. He turned to see a thin old crone in a Persian lamb stole gaping at him in fear and trembling. He began to stammer an explanation, but she sprang, as if rejuvenated, out of the alcove doorway, leaped past the new books and rushed out the front door, her stole waving a lazy, rich good-bye to literature and its denizens.

'My God,' said Hondorp to the voice. 'Look what you've done now. They'll be putting the white jacket on me.'

All reasoning sweetness, the voice said, 'I'll come clean. You've done your stint. Take a look up here.' Hondorp looked up. 'More to the right. That's it. Now what do you see?'

In the upper right-hand corner of the alcove, in a small space cleared of books, was a largish bulb that he hadn't noticed before. Shielding his eyes, he made out just behind it a large black box out of which stuck two glass circles, one of which was fitted to a short nozzle which seemed to be aimed at him.

'Get it?' asked the voice.

Hondorp studied a minute longer, then it came to him. 'Golk?'

'That-a-boy! You're On Camera.'

It was their slogan, their standard exposure, and in the voice's benevolent triumph, Hondorp recognized Golk's own voice.

It went on now, triumph doffed for conspiracy. 'Would you like to decoy the next victim for us?'

Hondorp shifted slowly from the first gear of his failure, torpor, into the second, malice. 'I'm with you,' he said. 'It'll be a pleasure.' He knew an ease he hadn't felt for some time.

The confrontation with Golk was the one for which more than any other he had somehow been prepared. He'd watched the show a good many times in the last few years, and the promise Golk made to all New York at the end of every programme, his long finger jabbing at them right through the camera with playful threat, 'Watch out. One of these days you'll be on camera too,' constituted for Hondorp one of the few contracts which he felt might be fulfilled for him, one of the fewer he looked forward to fulfilling. 'For my part, I go to the south,' he said out loud. He had been discovered.

'Haha, hoho, hughhugh, ohhh,' crackled the voice. 'Mahvellous.' And then, in another manner, direct, un-coloured: 'Crank it, boys. Now, victim.' Hondorp recognized the term from the programme—it stood for the unconscious participant in the scene or 'golk'—and did not take offence. He looked up to the camera nozzle. 'Take out that *Crusade in Europe* on the fourth shelf to your left. That's right. Ease out the little mike in back of it. That-a-boy. Our sound level's a little shaky. O.K. Slip it into the second shelf somewhere. That's right. Now hide the cord a little better behind the books.'

Hondorp eased, shifted, tucked, and hid; and did it while feeling that he was proceeding along his own grain. 'Where are you?' he asked.

'In a fish store across the street. I see you on a monitor. Now listen carefully. Here's our pitch,' and Golk's voice warmed with an intrigue which released thick roots into the ready soil of Hondorp's disappointments. 'Two shelves above that *Crusade in Europe*, no, more to the left. That's it. See that large book in the old binding, Lielies Noo-miz-mittiks'—this turned out to be Lyly's *Numismatics*—'that's it. Take it down.' Hondorp stretched and brought it down, shielding his head from a dust storm which didn't come. 'In the back binding, back cover, there's a slit with a piece of paper in it. Take it out.' Hondorp worked a fingernail into the binding and pulled out the paper. It was a dirty, ink-stained sheet of rough paper on which in a legible but exotic script he made out the following:

Acct. of Wm SHAXPER, ye GLOBE Thtr.	
2 ruffles	—2d
3 dblts.	—6d
rip in breeches, rpd	—2d
back accts.	—8d
Total	18d

O, what an ass (a fool, a rogue) and anguished knave am I,
Were it not monstrous that this player here
Were it not rotten that this actor here

At the bottom, the word 'Acknowledged' was scrawled, followed by a signature which Hondorp vaguely remembered as the one under the title-page illustration of his college copy of the *Works*. He trembled briefly with excitement.

'How's it look?' asked Golk.

'It'll fool a dupe,' said Hondorp pertly. 'Maybe even dupe a fool.' An indulgent chuckle from the wall.

'All right. Find one or the other. Here's the idea. Loosen your collar. Get some dust on yourself. All over. We'll have your suit cleaned. Try and work up a sweat. Look like some Shakespeare scholar who's found what you've found, but one who's too honest to just walk out with it and too poor to pay for the Noo-miz-mittiks.'

'I get it,' said Hondorp. He wiped his hand over the shelves and smeared it over his blue dacron.

'That's fine,' said the voice in the tone of that ironically benevolent authority which for long years now Hondorp had recognized as the world's real voice. 'Go on up to the front of the store, collar a likely victim, a browser type. Get him back here as quick as you can and give him the works. Don't worry about the owner. He's got our fifty bucks. The idea is you want to go halves with your man, he putting up the money to buy and you the scholarly know-how. The main thing is not to scare him until you get him back here on camera, but then give it to him hard and fast. It should take five or six minutes, ten at the most. We edit it later. When you've shot your bolt, we may give him the voice from the wall. Pretend not to hear it. Put the paper back in the book; it'll emphasize your scrupulousness, and give a little drama to the discovery.'

'I'm off,' said Hondorp, and he yanked at his tie, smeared another load of dust on his suit, and then loped out of the alcove, his head jerking with his version of scholarly excitement. He reared up at *Works of the Mind* and made a survey, six customers, and the little itchy-eyed proprietor who propelled an appealing, but fraternal, look at him. Two of the six were kids, a fifteen-year-old looking at the Modern Library, and a slightly younger girl half-way through a paper-back aphrodisiac. There were three middle-aged women in front of Biographies, Art, and New Fiction. The victim-to-be—Hondorp almost saw him spotlighted by victimage—was an obese, bearded coot inclined over a volume of engravings. Hondorp sidled up with an introductory cough. The Beard shifted a monstrous rear end to block the approach, but Hondorp leaned over the obstruction and whispered that he would like to speak to him about something of great importance.

The Beard closed the book and turned with dignity. 'Sir?' he said, a dull boom from the guts that drew stares and shushes from the other readers.

Hondorp bent to the Beard's level and whispered, 'I have made what I think is a discovery of first-class importance in an old volume I just found in Alcove B, and I must discuss it with someone other than the proprietor.'

The Beard's eyes dilated with terror; Hondorp hurried on: 'May I show it to you? I can hardly believe my own eyes, and after looking here, I realized that you would be the only one capable of confirming what I've seen. If you aren't interested, I shall try the woman at Biographies, but it will be second-best.'

'All right,' said the Beard, modulating the boom to a room-shaking whisper. 'I can give you a minute.' He drew out a dollar pocket watch, held it at arm's length in front of him, and then followed it and Hondorp into the alcove. 'In that one,' said Hondorp, pointing to the *Numismatics*. He pulled the book down, opened it, and drew out the paper.

'Look at this and see if you make of it what I did.' He handed it over with grandeur.

The Beard looked, removed the spectacles he used for pictures, and replaced them with a pair which seemed to consume his irises. He himself was consumed by ravenous contemplation. When he bent his head back to look at Hondorp, he was shivering. 'Must be a joke,' he said.

'Elizabethan calligraphy is not my speciality,' said Hondorp, 'but I have done some work in it. I should be inclined to say that the signature before us dates from no later than 1630, the paper as well. The ink is not perhaps as faded as one might expect, but the variations in documents are astonishing. I remember a thirteenth-century codex I spent a day with at the Vatican, and I swear to you by all that's holy, I thought I could discern the dampness of the ink, so clear and fresh it was. My feeling is that we have hit upon the genuine article.'

'Did they have laundry lists?' asked the Beard, his boom crippled by awe.

'Apparently.'

'My God,' rumbled the Beard. 'We've found something.' Hondorp's face flickered with triumph. The Beard's great eyes bugged, aflare with suspicion. 'Why didn't you pocket it?'

'Pocket it? Without remunerating the bookseller? You must be joking. That's why I've come to you. I haven't any money. And we have to pay him for this. I shall share the discovery and whatever profit there may be with you.'

The Beard was grave. 'That's commendable. Very proper. A rarity in young—', he appraised Hondorp, 'younger men. And I'm going to reward you for your instincts of probity. The paper is of course a forgery, but I'm going to give you five dollars for it anyway. And I'll buy that book there to

16

recompense the bookseller. The anecdote will be worth the money. Perhaps I'll have it framed.'

Hondorp fixed with cold eye the swindling lips. 'Sir,' he said icily. 'The paper you hold in your hand may well be worth fifty thousand dollars. Or more. It may be priceless. We must give the bookseller one hundred dollars for the *Numismatics*. We'll tell him that it's more valuable than his price indicates. Let's see what he's asking.' Hondorp looked on the back flap. 'Forty-five cents.' He frowned at this lapse in Golk's strategy: even the poorest scholar would be expected to have that price in his pocket. 'Then we take the document up to the Forty-Second Street Library or to Columbia. And tomorrow, the world.'

The Beard switched spectacles, and from the comparative clarity of the initial pair, poured pity and scorn upon Hondorp. 'You are a most generous man, sir. With my money. After all, a laundry slip and a line or two of verse do not constitute a new play. Dirty drawers are dirty drawers, Shakespeare's or yours, sir.' Chuckle-boom. 'I suggest that we offer the owner four dollars and fifty cents, ten times the asked-for price. He will be delighted without being suspiciously mystified.'

'You may be right,' said Hondorp thoughtfully.

The two were huddled together in criminal fellowship working out the details of their scheme, when Golk's voice came over the speaker, 'Robber.'

The Beard staggered. 'What did you say?'

'I said nothing,' said Hondorp.

The Beard stared around fiercely. 'Robber,' thundered Golk. The Beard's face grew cavernous with terror. He spun, shook a great fist at Hondorp and boomed, 'Trickster. Lousy liar. Rat. Criminal. Swindler. Bum,' and he was off with a galloping waddle past the tables, down the stairs, out of the door and down the street.

Golk's roar filled the alcove. 'Crank it, boys. A splendid golk. You were splendid, victim. What's your name?'

Hondorp told him.

'You were splendid, Hondorp.'

'Thank you,' said Hondorp. The commendation stirred him not a little.

'Come on across the street,' said Golk. 'Hirsch's Fish Store.'

'All right,' said Hondorp. 'How about the mike? Shall I bring the mike?' He could hardly credit his eagerness to help out.

'No, no, friend. Never mind. We'll clear up. You've done your part splendidly. Just shoot over here.'

II

Hondorp, out on the kerb waiting to cross the street, saw through the glass pane of the fish market the great bare dome he knew as Golk's. It was propped over a scarp of dry ice on which gleamed the sad carcasses of numberless fish. Golk seemed part and parcel of the display, a monster specimen who'd disgorged the others. The chameleon knack, the rare trick of being one's environment, this was Golk's most unusual gift as an actor in his own scenes. What one would have sworn was an absolutely uncamouflageable skull had passed over New York as that of a race tout, corporation lawyer, Bombay Yogi, ex-prelim middleweight, lion-tender, pickpocket, Belgian poet, and God knows what else.

As Hondorp walked in, the fish turned human, straightened, and clapped him on the shoulder. 'Good man, Hondorp friend,' it said, and smiled the warmest welcome Hondorp had ever been accorded.

There were three other men in the store, one in a white apron, the owner, and two others dressed like Golk in slacks and sport shirts. One, a tough type with a scaphoid head (nose for prow, dipping chin), kneeled by a large tape recorder hooked into an audio panel filled with patch cords and dial knobs. Two of the cords were strung up the wall across the ceiling and out the top of the front door. The other man, a kind of swollen ganglion, was packing up a large camera, unscrewing attachment after attachment and stowing each one in a black suitcase.

'That's Fitch,' said Golk, flapping a hand towards the former. 'Our cameraman. The other's Benson, the audio man. We have a floorman up in the bookstore attic. This here's Mr—what's your name again, friend?' Golk asked the owner.

'Hirsch.'

'Mr Hirsch, who's made himself a small pile for his afternoon's disturbance. Am I wrong, Hirsch?'

'No, it's been good,' said Hirsch. 'A Tuesday by me's a lousy day.'

Hondorp nodded to Hirsch, and said 'How do you do?' to Fitch and Benson. They said nothing; the owner said that he was fine.

'Don't bother with them,' said Golk. 'They're beyond the amenities. Technicians, you know. A way of life.' Hondorp nodded to endorse the view and winced to see Benson dip into the nasal hold of his ship for a boogie, roll it up, and flip it absently towards Hirsch. 'I never wanted to be an engineer,' he said thoughtfully.

'So,' said Golk, turning his face up to Hondorp's, 'what's the reaction?'

Hondorp knew that this question would have consequences for him. 'It was,' he said after a between-the-stirrups-and-the-ground calculation, 'like someone taking off the top of my head and peering in.' Golk's face quivered with what Hondorp took for either an approving frown or smiling disapproval. 'Like meeting destiny,' he went on, less securely. The frown almost took over. 'Like being shot out of a cannon without knowing you were even in one.' Smile routed frown.

'You were cool, friend. You were really cool. It was great to see. You're not an actor by some lousy chance?'

By no chance, happy or otherwise, was he an actor, said Hondorp.

'Naturally. No actor could have pulled it off the way you did. There aren't five actors in New York can appear on a spontaneous programme, outside of an interview about themselves. And they're unemployed. You think on your feet. You got gall. I like that. And then being cool. I like that better.'

Hondorp took the praise as a spinnaker takes wind, but held a part detached waiting for the sequence, for what counted. Would it turn out to be only money? Or, worse, was Golk's praise *it*?

Golk was looking him over, hair to feet, a meat inspector without the jabbing thumb. 'Now what is your line, Hondorp?'

This time it was easier: Hondorp sensed it would be one of his last trials on the charge. 'I'm between jobs.'

Golk nodded, and called back to Fitch. 'What'd I tell you? Three o'clock on a Tuesday afternoon and an able-bodied man prowling around a bookstore. I knew we'd pick one up here.' His fish-blue eyes were on Hondorp's dull chocolate ones. 'I thought right away you might be one of us.'

Hondorp tensed, ready to leg it out at a gallop, his eyes covering Fitch and Benson. In New York City you could never tell when you were going to get it, who would do it, when it would take place. But no one moved, so he asked, 'What's the pitch?'

'This,' said Golk, monumentally, and he whirled, and started chugging back and forth in the ten square feet of floor space, dragging Hirsch's and Hondorp's swivelling eyes after him. This for a minute, then full-stop, and he tilted his rocky dome towards Hondorp's chin. 'We're a small, swinging, independent outfit. We've had a tight grip on local time for over five years, and we're right now on the verge of cracking network. We're a close bunch; we work like this—' he raised an unspaced index and second finger. 'The work is pleasant, and more than that, the money a fistful more than you've ever looked at, and you can quit on notice. You join AFTRA, and we pay the dues. That's all the entanglements you need. What do you say?'

Now that it was at last here, Hondorp nearly wasn't. He felt himself sinking into the huge blue bulges of Golk's eyes. Fish smells seeped into him, and they seemed to rot out the unformed but ruling notions of Hondorp's careerless life, his endless, unpressured leisure. 'I'm not fit,' he said, half-entranced. 'I'm not ready.' He felt Golk's hand tight on his forearm, and he came up for air. 'I've got no skills. I'm nothing but an ex-poly-sci. major.'

Golk held him hard. 'We know what we want, Hondorp. We'll make your skills for you. You've got all it takes to start right now. Tomorrow at the Parisak Building. We'll be waiting for you.'

'We'll be waiting,' echoed a shattering baritone that sent Hondorp back hard against a display case. (Benson had called through a loudspeaker.)

'So watch it,' said Hirsch sharply. 'For fifty fish you don't need to break up the business.'

'Maybe,' said Hondorp, somehow feeling Hirsch's

message was the most important that had got through to him.

Golk's short strong arm moved him out of the store into the sun. 'Take it easy now, my friend. Being one of us, we don't want you getting busted by a truck. Want some cab fare?' Hondorp shook his head. 'Well here then,' said Golk, and he slipped something into Hondorp's palm. 'Take the Independent home. That's the prescription for you today. Ha, ha, ha. We'll be expecting you.'

Hondorp walked off down the street, one fist tight around the subway token.

III

Hondorp announced the great news to his father, not that same night—Poppa Hondorp dined in front of the television set and from then on heard nothing that was not electronically transmitted—but next morning. Breakfast was Poppa Hondorp's hour for communication with his son, or, at least, that part of the meal which followed his reading of the headlines and obituary columns and the drinking of a second cup of coffee spiked with dousings of cigar ash. The sessions with the obituaries prepared Poppa Hondorp for those who had not yet made their way into them: his son, his patients—he was an ear, nose, and throat man—and what he called 'city riffraff'. The obituaries were Poppa Hondorp's measure of human worth. 'There's little they can add or subtract from you then,' was his view. Poppa's eye had sharpened over the years so that he could weigh a two-and-a-half-inch column of ex-alderman against three and a quarter inches of inorganic chemist and know at a glance their comparative worth. When his son had one day suggested that the exigencies of the printer and make-up man might in part account for the amount of space accorded a deceased, Poppa Hondorp had shivered with a rage his son knew he should never excite again. 'Don't mess with credos,' knew young Hondorp, so the obituaries were sacrosanct; the *Times* issued mysteriously from an immaculate source.

If the obituaries assessed primarily what Poppa Hondorp called 'public men', private men, such as himself, were best assessed by the attendance at their funeral rites. It was one of Poppa's great, and well-founded, fears that his own rites would be but sparsely attended.

His other chief fear was related to the first: relying on patients rather than friends for mourners, Poppa Hondorp located the warmth of all friendship, the attention of all kinfolk, the love of human beings and humanity itself, in his only child. His absorption had led to young Hondorp's status: all of his thirty-seven years, but the two which he had spent in Texas and North Carolina army camps during the war, had been spent at home, and except for the private's pay he had drawn in those years, he had never earned a penny of his own. His total dependence was the cornerstone of his father's security.

Since the death of his wife nearly twenty years ago, Poppa Hondorp's being had been founded on the fact that his substance was vouched for by the needlessness of his son's having any. That his son provided a sounding-board for his opinions, silent companionship to his TV revels, and the only complete and familiar human form he knew (he regarded others as little more than appendages to the ears and respiratory tract) was incidental to this monumental function.

It was Hondorp's knowledge of what he meant to his father that led to the break which he announced at breakfast. Hondorp broke out of the cocoon for the sake of breaking the earthly peace it gave his father. He had no conscious desire other than this, no desire to do anything than what he had for years been doing, wandering over New York, regarding the products of the earth and the masterpieces of the ages. But through all the years, the break with his father had been waiting its occasion, and now it was with glee that he went to it, with fearsome glee, but with glee. It was the classic, primal action: all else would stem from it.

At the table he listened to the unholy music of his father's ingurgitation of the ash-loaded coffee, and thought, 'This is the last day.' And then, at the first pause in the oral mayhem, he said, 'Poppa. I was offered a job yesterday, and I'm going to take it.'

Poppa Hondorp slowly lifted his great white head, and his son watched the eyes widen as if they were the object of a tug-of-war. A gurgle that seemed to start at the bottom of Poppa Hondorp's feet worked its way up through the throat and issued forth as a moan. Poppa Hondorp was looking into an abyss where, a second before, he had seen only his son. It was too much. He drifted into a reverie unfissured by catastrophe. The oblivion lasted less than a minute, and when Poppa Hondorp came to, he came to living with a changed world. He managed to meet it with dignity. 'So what,' he asked his son, 'is this possibility of yours?'

Hondorp told him what had happened in the bookstore and, later, in Hirsch's market.

'Golk, Golk, Golk,' pronounced Poppa Hondorp, and the name shook his dignity and led him to make one of his forthright appraisals. 'A two-inch junk-dealer. I've seen his lousy show a half a million times.'

'It's an amusing programme, Poppa,' said his son with a firmness and courtesy that surprised hearer even more than speaker.

'*Schweine* laugh at dung.'

Hondorp had watched his father roar, drool, bend, bulge, and collapse at Golk's programme, as at any other show officially billed as comedy. But he asked, 'Are you sure you remember the show, Poppa?'

'Bald man passing himself off as something or other on gullible riffraff. Half a million times I've watched the lousy dung.'

'He's a clever guy, Poppa.'

'Clever at junk. At dung. Junk is junk; dung dung. Cleverness counts nothing. What counts is force, distinction, heart, not pushing slobs in the head with pie in the mouth. If this clever punk of yours makes two inches in the *Times*, I'll have half of Central Park West at my rites.' To this he added, after a moment, 'P.G.' for 'Please God'.

'May that time be many, many years off, Poppa.'

Poppa Hondorp propped his cigar—a dud missile—against his cup, and stared at it mournfully. Then he spoke to his son gently as if tucking him into his words. 'And what does this Golk wish you to do for him, darling?'

'Assist. I'm to be part of the crew. There'll be a number of functions.'

Poppa Hondorp let his head sway back and forth. 'But my dear,' he said sweetly, 'what can you do? What have you learned to do? The political science. Ask yourself, where can you fit into a complex organization? You are—at the very most—a student of life, not a worker in it.' Poppa Hondorp got up from the table and went up to the dining-room windows between which, on the wall strip, was fixed an aneroid barometer cased in mahogany by Hammacher Schlemmer. Poppa Hondorp opened the glass face and moved the hands together. 'Fair in the sky, but stormy *bei* Hondorp,' he said quietly. He stared out the windows across Central Park towards the stone tip of Cleopatra's Needle. 'There is so much in the world to study,' he said, and he sighted beyond the figured tip to the South Wing of the Metropolitan Museum. 'So much, and you, my darling, have the rare opportunity of, in this life, studying it. But no, what do you want to do? Push your nose into a lousy routine, bind yourself hand and foot, leg and thigh, truss yourself up in misery, in a way of life of which you'll never know from nothing.'

'I can always quit, Poppa,' said Hondorp quietly, trying to cope with the rising headwind.

'True, but spare yourself that. Stop now. Don't go.'

Hondorp saw that there was nothing more to be done. He got up, folded his napkin, and started down the hall. His father asked him with some firmness where he was going.

'Bathroom,' answered Hondorp. *Bei* Hondorp, this destination took precedence over all others, trivial or mortal.

Hondorp locked the door, sat on the toilet seat, and studied the floor's black squares islanded in the white, his favourite backdrop for reflection. He stayed put until he heard his father call out, 'Good-bye, darling. Have a nice day.' And then, more quietly, 'I hope this evening will see you in a better frame of mind. Restored to—to——' and he drifted off.

Hondorp called out, 'Good-bye, Poppa,' listened to his father's farewell to the cook, the door slam, and his own sigh of relief.

IV

For Hondorp, moving around the city had been one of the great ends of life. Having no place to go, going itself was what counted, his pleasure, his occupation. When he didn't walk, he went by bus, the Eighth Avenue bus from the apartment house door, and then by successive transfers as far around the city as an afternoon's hours and the day's desire permitted.

Mostly he walked, down Central Park West or through the park itself, and then, if he didn't make his afternoon in the park—at the zoo, or watching the ballplayers, or talking to the governesses whom he'd come to know over the years—he'd move on farther down the East Side avenues past the great houses, museums and libraries, and past the thousand shops whose commerce had been for years in no small part his own.

Today his walk was an occasion: he had a destination, and for Hondorp, destination was almost destiny. The walk which altered his life was taken therefore in a spirit of dedication. Elegy as well: Hondorp regarded the green ovals and bridle paths and bushes, the castle, the bird sanctuary, the lake, and the glowing monsters of the avenues with the sad eyes of farewell.

Central Park was his own; he knew it as a dog knows its master's backyard, every step and shrub of it. As a boy, Hondorp had thought of the park as an immense wood, one large enough to contain all necessary adventure. The day its dimensions withered for him was one of the most important in his life: a patient of his father's had told him that he owned a ranch in Nevada in which fifty Central Parks could be hidden like needles in a haystack. The law of proportions had burst furiously upon Hondorp, and with it the consequence that other people's values were not his, need not be his. Unformulated, but tenacious, the law was the groundwork for his years of hibernation.

Helped by an incident. The night he had heard the withering news, he decided, for no reason apparent to him, to conduct an experiment with his goldfish. For two years he had maintained a bowlful of the graceful, inexpressive creatures, daily crumbling wafers of nourishment, changing their water, watching their endless, pathetic circumnavigations. That night he decided that they were beneath the care he gave them, useful only for experiment. Each day he put one less flake into the bowl, until, in a week's time, the less enterprising fish began to starve. There were ten of them to begin with; in a month they were all flushed down the toilet. For the first few days, he had feared and relished the suicidal guilt of the assassin. Then it was over.

Now today, thirty years after, walking down through the park, he felt a kindred feeling. In the huge, mysterious thrust of the little park towards spring, he felt a corresponding thrust in himself away from that hibernated self which had been his father's as well as his own. And an aspect of his thrust—as of nature's—was patricidal.

CHAPTER TWO

I

THE Parisak Building was one of the glassy boxes which, in the nineteen forties and fifties, began turning Manhattan into a kind of open-air bazaar, a transparent hive of commuting drones. It constituted the single important architectural stopgap to the entertainment industry's flight towards the West Coast, and was thus a gesture as prodigal and as useless as most of the imperial gestures of post-war New York. It took up a full city block and displaced twenty-six stories' worth of East River air. Its architects had tried to imply a relationship between it and the slender, taller UN Secretariat Building across the way, but had contrived only the sinister appearance of a crouching beast camouflaged to look like its neighbour in order to devour it. Inside the rose-tinted, air-conditioned, environment-proof bulk reigned the modern architectural trinity, cleanliness, spaciousness, and luminosity. Inside and out, abstract design, which would have been equally suitable in a bank, a mortuary, or a five-hundred-family house, testified in its anonymous power to the rule of the species, of the institution.

The Parisak's particular function was further disguised by a one-acre hothouse garden which, along with two immense information desks that curved toward each other like a pair of smiling lips, composed the entire contents of the ground floor, another prodigal gesture of the age's collective opulence. Here, approaching the lower aluminium lip, Hondorp, dark and tubular, his habitual air of depression not seriously relieved by a blue-ribboned straw hat, confronted the free-floating brilliance of a female smile which so discomposed him that a second passed before he could remember what he was doing there.

'Golk,' he recalled.

The smile crumpled, and a voice as smooth as hair tonic murmured, 'I beg your pardon.'

Hondorp articulated his want, and the smile bloomed, a bright eye glanced at a gold-lettered index, and the hair tonic whispered, 'Nine-sixty-seven. I only know the Network people by heart.'

'I understand,' said Hondorp sweetly. 'Are there elevators?' He could see nothing but the glass-walled garden and some blue steel pillars which supported a distant twinkling ceiling.

'Right through the air-curtain to the garden, and up the escalators.'

Hondorp started to say 'Thank you', but realized it would be like thanking a record which supplies the day's weather report. He made his way through the odorous but invisible curtain to what looked for a moment like five silver rivers flowing, miraculously, uphill. He stepped into one of the streams and was catapulted up while a voice from the handrail informed him that he was enjoying the second-fastest escalator ride in the world.

'What would the first be?' wondered Hondorp.

'. . . the Prudential Building in Chicago's Loop,' said the handrail.

At the top, a uniformed midget directed him to a mirrored cell which rocketed him to the ninth floor. He stepped out into what seemed sheer space. This effect, the realized fantasy of a futurist, yielded as his eyes adjusted to the shy colours which worked to hide the sleek corridors which filed starlike off a tiny gold reception desk to his right. At the desk, a weary blonde in what Hondorp recognized as the Parisak uniform and smile asked him whom he wished to see.

'Mr Golk.'

'All the way down Alley C,' she said with a mournfulness that conjured in Hondorp visions of weekly funerals. He moved down the third corridor. At his back he heard a click and buzz; the blonde was releasing a switchboard key in a tiny gold board by her desk.

'All the way down' meant a fifty-second walk past a series of numbered oak doors which shut out sound as well as light from the corridor. The silence was astonishing.

The door numbered '967' at first seemed to be set off from the undeviating row; it had for Hondorp the air of an alcove, and thus, unlike the other doors, of one that was made for entrances more than for exits. But his knock brought no response, nor did a second and third knock. He turned a delicate brass knob and walked in.

Cacophony. Hondorp put his hand to his heart. 'The other side of the moon,' he thought, and then, in adjusting to it, saw that the noise was the ordinary one of six or seven people typing and talking in a forty-by-forty, high-ceilinged room so packed with a jungle of equipment, desks, backdrops, pulleys, screens, cameras and unidentifiable objects that Hondorp thought it must be a kind of attic for the building, the secret closet of some disorderly history.

Two of the people—Hondorp saw in one the ship's head he knew as Fitch—were holding a film strip to the light, arguing about it and pointing at each other with cutting shears. A man in overalls was cranking a sighting machine and staring through an eyepiece at what he cranked. The mode of all the activity, sighting, typing, cutting, was unremitting absorption. Nobody looked up at Hondorp; nobody looked at anyone doing anything else. It was the obverse of the isolation Hondorp had felt in the corridor; it was isolation from distraction, and yet the isolation was not without invitation.

Off the main room were five or six ancillary ones, odd growths from the larger one. Hondorp sidled into the first growth on his right, and of the man reading a *Batman* comic book with holy fervour he asked for Golk. There was no response. 'These people seem unused to polite society,' thought Hondorp. He asked again, and a cherubic face touched at the mouth with chocolate smears looked up and asked what he thought of Golk dressed like Batman flying in through the window of some kindergarten.

'Sounds fine,' said Hondorp, 'but where's Golk?'

A hairy little arm pointed across the large room. 'Thanks,' said Hondorp, and went out dodging desks and cranes. He entered a cranny where a gorgeous Negress was typing furiously. Behind the cranny was a kind of cave and into this the girl waved Hondorp, without looking up from the machine.

Inside, Golk sat at a dagger-shaped desk. In the dimness, he seemed little more than a bare skull, the surviving dome of a city sunk into the Golden Horn. The skull tilted up towards a monitor just above the cave's entrance. Still looking up at it, Golk gestured to Hondorp, not apparently to take a seat, as there was only one in the office, and he was in it, but as some vestige of imperial hospitality. 'So here you are,' he said gently, eyes still on the screen.

'Yes, I'm here,' said Hondorp, and he took off his boater, fidgeting with an uneasiness compounded of anxiety, fear, and excitement, exacerbated rather than soothed by the gentle welcome. He turned round to the screen and the uneasiness became shock as he saw the image of his own consternated face filling the convexity.

'Now that's a fine expression,' said Golk. He clicked a key, and the image disappeared. For a second, Hondorp felt he'd been turned to smoke. 'I've been watching you since the receptionist announced you were here. You've got a great face, man. A great TV face.'

'Thank you,' said Horndorp, slowly, sincerely.

'It's expressive without being too mobile. There are a lot worse faces drawing two hundred thousand fish a year.'

'I haven't been on another programme, have I?' asked Hondorp, putting nothing past Golk and trying to remember whether he'd scratched himself on the way down the hall.

'Of course not,' said Golk. 'I was just getting in some practice.'

'Practice?'

'Practice. I work on faces.' This was said with some self-satisfaction.

'Well, well,' said Hondorp, feeling that Golk's smug tone gave him the first sniff of advantage he'd had with him. 'I've spent not a little time doing that myself. It's pleasant work, not as easy as the unobservant might think. Of course, I've studied lots of other things at the same time. I'm a—' and suddenly he saw that he'd not only lost his advantage but was again the victim under observation. He completed the sentence to himself 'scholar'.

'I don't mind scholarly types,' said Golk, and Hondorp trembled at the telepathy. Golk's eyes were like blue suns, and Hondorp felt them shrivelling what they regarded. 'I'm a doer myself, but a man must fuel up with thought. That I know. Few know that like I know it. I'm glad to have scholar-types around me.'

As if a coin had been pushed through a slit in his head, Hondorp found words tumbling out of him. 'It's wrong to think of scholars as idlers, very wrong. The Latin word for such activity, for such intense leisure is *otium*, and business, busyness, was just the negative of this, *neg-otium*. The doer, the busy-man is just the negative.'

'Clever, those Romans,' put in Golk.

'The Greeks had it too, but I don't remember the words.'

'Let me know when you can,' said Golk gently, but his eyes were so far away from the request that Hondorp pulled up short. 'I've got to watch it,' he told himself. He looked at Golk's head poised in the air as if he were tuning in on a distant frequency. Hondorp started to ask if he could be of help but Golk held up his hand. 'We're just about to show your golk. Want to golk it?'

'Look at it?'

'To look with the critical eye,' defined Golk without smiling. 'Verb transitive.'

'I better just look at it,' said Hondorp, feeling the energy of self-assertion returning after the introductory shake-up.

Golk spotted the independence and seemed to approve it. At least he said, 'That's proper. Let's go,' and Hondorp followed him out to the main room, where ten or twelve people—most of them those Hondorp had seen—sat on the floor facing a large screen. Golk led him over by the arm. 'These are the golks,' he said. 'Noun improper.' The characterization was apparently familiar to the others; at least it stirred no response but Golk's own cackle. 'This is Hendricks,' he said. A lanky, nervous beauty in slacks and moccasins held out her hand to Hondorp. 'This is Hondorp,' said Golk. 'You alliterate.'

'Golk's a great pointer-outer,' said Hendricks in a low, raw voice.

'I've seen you somewhere,' said Hondorp partly in a jab at the social manner, partly in simple truth. 'We haven't met, for I'd have remembered, but I've seen you.' He smiled, thinking his gallantry successful, and thus cancelling the small success it had.

'Out in the sun with Keller and DiMaggio maybe,' said the cherubic reader of *Batman*. 'I'm Klebba,' he said. 'Veddy Klebba as a matter of fact.' He flapped out a thick palm which Hondorp took and shook.

'We're a circle of wits,' said Hendricks. 'And anything new so disconcerts us that we can't shut our holes. Don't let us worry you.'

'Perhaps,' said Hondorp inappropriately. Then he shook hands with Fitch and Benson, who smiled with a rudimentary sort of recognition, then with a small, lean man named Pegram, and with Elaine, the Negress, whose style, he saw now, had been modelled, and with no small success, on Lena Horne's. His hand was in the air for another shake when the fluorescent lights overhead blinked out, and an eight-by-ten screen slid down from the ceiling and was illuminated by beams shot from a projection booth in back. Golk, seated in the armchair, throned above his followers, had clicked the switches which had wrought these changes, and then clicked another which caused the screen to fill with a view of Follett's Bookstore.

Hondorp found a place on the floor and stared as the screen showed him his own image, tall, loose, slightly sinister, not the self he thought he knew, the inconspicuous but assured, lean, springy, delicately-tamed leopard of the New York streets. There he was, his face pointed like a revolver against the pyramid of Sagans, and then there was a cut to the alcove with the voice asking him whether he was 'looking or buying'. When his image responded, Hondorp curled like an ash. His voice, passing now directly to his ears instead of being modified by his cranial bones, was that of a vituperative whiner, a wavery sac of acid. It wrenched a groaning shudder from him.

'What's the matter?' asked Golk. 'Don't like the close-up?'

'I don't much like it,' said Klebba as the scene rolled on. 'Nor the first two-shot.'

'Why not?' asked Golk, eyes hard on the screen.

'They're both held thirty frames too long.'

'All right. Slice them five or six,' said Golk with a permissive ease that brought from Hondorp a grunt of surprise.

'What a critic,' said Golk to him. 'You got to be more articulate, man.'

The scene rolled on through an enfilade of objections by Klebba, Benson, and Pegram, to all of which Golk seemed to yield. 'What a harmony here,' thought Hondorp, but this reflection was broken into by something brushing against his leg. He shifted away, then felt the same sensation. He turned to see what touched him; it was another leg, a very beautiful one. After momentary contemplation of it, Hondorp reached down and stroked it. The leg stayed. He kept his palm on the knee as on the shift knob of an old car, ready to move, although by now it was clear that the contact was not accidental. The leg was as informative as a letter of intentions. Hondorp's eye trailed back along the leg until it met Elaine's, which was still more informative. Coupled with the revelation of his screen face and soundtrack voice, the information promoted in him an agitation which made him groan with visions of possibility.

'Come now man,' said Golk. 'Speak up. Is the audio too low for you?'

'It's just fine,' said Hondorp, and he turned again to Elaine's lush, come-hither face, so frank it seemed a burlesque of what it offered. And what it offered suddenly decomposed Hondorp, and he remembered a moment of similar decomposition which centred about his first sexual encounter, an agonizing walk he had taken up and down Forty-fourth Street outside Walgreen's steeling himself to go inside to ask for the indispensable, protective article.

Finally, he'd forced himself up to the drug counter, surrendered his turn to a woman who'd come in after him, and then requested the prophylactic by one of its vulgar names.

'Large packet or small?' the clerk had asked.

'Small,' he'd said, sure that it was the desire of experience rather than the experience of desire that counted for him. The clerk reached under the counter, brought out a little blue packet and asked if he should wrap it.

'No,' said Hondorp, and tucked it away in his wallet.

'I think these will suit you nicely,' said the clerk, a fruity-looking banterer. 'Will there be anything else today?'

'No,' Hondorp had replied, a rage of sweat breaking on his face.

He was eighteen and two days before had been at his mother's funeral. It was there at his first experience of human mortality that he'd decided to experience the other crucial human engagement. Things happened rarely to Hondorp, but when they happened, they happened in bunches and were greeted with the sweat of his brow.

He sweated now on the floor of the screening room. 'It's just too much for me,' was his thought. 'There's just too much going on.'

This appraisal was saluted by the crack of what seemed like doom itself to him. The screening was over, and Golk had clicked the chair switch. 'Let there be light,' said Klebba.

'*Fiat lux*,' muttered Hondorp, his memory careening again, this time towards his ex-Latin-teacher mother who had supplied the acidic drip which scrawled Roman phrases across the pleasures of his youth.

'Speak up,' said Klebba, breaking into the fattish, spiteful image crowding Hondorp. The assault was joined by Golk's boom, 'How'd you like it, Hondorp?'

Hondorp controlled himself and managed, 'A little disconcerting, but quite amusing.'

'Yes,' said Golk dourly, his bare dome sidling highlights into Hondorp's eyes. 'Amusement seems to be our limit here. From your damn groans I couldn't tell whether you were in anguish or jerking off.' Hondorp felt the blood run in his cheeks. 'Well, maybe we'll do a little bit more than amuse people before we're through.' He turned to Pegram. 'Where're we shooting this afternoon?'

'Central Park. The chess and checkers golk.'

'That's right,' said Golk. 'You come along too, Hondorp. You'll see how we work from the back of the store this time. If you get any ideas for golks, note them down. Hendricks will whip you into shape as far as the general layout around here goes. You've come in at a crucial time. In five weeks we go on network. Summer replacement for Borgeler. If we make out, we're in, and you'll be making five times the money you're making now, or sixty-five thousand times what you made before. And that's not all. We may be able to stick up there. Borgeler's brand of crap has shot its wad.' On this involved figure, Golk spun and headed back for his cave. To Hondorp, it seemed as if the lights had been turned off again in the room.

'All right,' said Hendricks, touching his elbow with one of the longest forefingers he'd ever seen. 'I'll show you the hawks and handsaws.'

II

Hendricks led Hondorp out of the Parisak Building and across the street to an old brownstone which stood more solidly in its stubbly isolation than the soaring commercial future of the area seemed to warrant. An elevator rattled them to the top floor, and they stepped out on to a large flagstone terrace shaded by a triangular blue awning. Here and there in nooks contrived by perversely pruned shrubs and five or six scarlet maples were twenty-five or thirty tables. The terrace gave on the upper reaches of the Queensborough Bridge, and except for the UN Building on its right and the Parisak Building on its left, the view was air, sun, and sky. In New York, this amounted to pastoral seclusion.

Hondorp, fresh from his experience with the Parisak greenery, was unsure what the brownstone's function was. If it was a restaurant, he decided that it was by far the nicest he had been in. He wasn't sure that it was, however, until he saw four men moving around in tuxedos with faintly coloured auxiliary seams which established them as uniforms. They were the least waiter-like waiters he had ever seen, bearing the silver trays as if to their lovers' bedsides. The head waiter—no auxiliary seams, no trays—came to them with fraternal smile, whispering 'Good afternoon, good afternoon,' and brought them to a table on the east end of the awning.

'Very nice,' said Hondorp with what he felt was the properly tentative manner of the professional New Yorker discovering another tolerable 'place'.

The 'nice' included the table as well as the restaurant. When he repeated it, the approval extended to Hendricks as well. Hondorp, although he habitually paid no compliments, made almost no gestures which could figure in any conceivable scheme of gallantry, did have a genuine nose for style in the ways and places and people of the city, and it was clear to him that Hendricks, slacks, moccasins, and all, was a person of complex style.

She sat at right angles to him, her profile clear against a deep blue sky, a long, barely curved forehead unbroken by a coiffure which pulled her yellow, moon-coloured hair straight back, a brief, slightly puffy nose, and an oval jaw which both framed and rounded out the rest. It was a rare, fine face which, for Hondorp, loomed large, a topography that his eye explored as a climber might a river valley far below him. His survey finished at a sharp flick on his earlobe.

'Wake up,' she said. 'You look as if you're trying to guess my weight.'

'Sorry,' he said coldly, massaging the tingling lobe.

'I ordered a Riesling. All right?'

'Of course,' said Hondorp, wondering whether this would be beer, soup, or fish.

By the time he found out, he was confronted with the challenge of a sixteen-inch polygot menu, the perusal of which gave him precious little insight into anything but the vastness of another world which up till now had hardly existed for him. Cuisine *bei* Hondorp centred about prime chunks of a few staples, and pleasure was a function of how much one managed to stuff away without immediate ill-consequence. The menu loomed like another landscape for him. He faced it by ordering, in quite excellent and confident French, an item under each of three rubrics.

'You're not much of a trencherman, I see,' said Hendricks. She ordered a roast-beef sandwich, a cup of Chase and Sanborn coffee, and an apple. Hondorp deposited this refinement against future opportunities with such menus.

'What about my "whipping in"?' he asked.

'That's nonsense. He just wanted me to keep you company. There's nothing you can learn. There are six standard lenses on TV cameras in New York, but we use ordinary movie cameras. A "two-shot" is a shot of two people, but that's for cameramen. "Crossrows" has to do with inserted film-clips, but we don't employ them.'

'How did you learn about them?'

'I spent tedious hours around the studios. Also I read up when I first came on the job. The technical side of our programme is very special, and not very difficult. In fact, the whole idea is kind of special.'

'What is the idea?' asked Hondorp. 'A kind of *Miss Lonelyhearts*, isn't it? Little views of people's problems seen by the sympathetic camera eye?'

Hendricks said 'No' very quickly, then thought a moment, and said it again. 'No, it's somewhat more abstract than that. Golk doesn't really feel for people. You'll see. Every once in a while he comes up with a new brand of golk and then he talks about it. You can take or leave what he says, but it's not a bit like *Miss Lonelyhearts*. I think I've seen him really sympathetic towards the victim only once or twice in the two and a half years I've been around.'

The waiter put before Hondorp a plate of cracked ice into which ten or twelve shells stuffed with little fatty objects were stuck, and at his recoil, said, 'You did order *moules*, didn't you sir?'

'I did,' said Hondorp. He extracted one of the molluscs with the silver tines of a utensil he'd never before used, put it into his mouth and winced again. 'Oh God,' he thought. 'Is it all worth it?'

'It's like staying in the sun too long your first day at the shore,' said Hendricks, and Hondorp stared, wondering if he'd actually said what he'd thought. 'You'll get used to it in a few days.'

'Maybe I move my lips,' thought Hondorp, 'and these Golk-types get some kind of training reading them.'

Hendricks reached for one of his shells and sucked out the mussel. 'I'm a food-moocher,' she said in what Hondorp spotted with happiness as her first concession to a style to which he could feel superior. He managed a facial twist of benign distaste. Its success—Hendricks responded in kind—somewhat restored his confidence.

'You know,' he said, deciding to do the leading, 'I really have seen you before. And not just passing by in the street, although I might have remembered you even then. You are different from people one passes in the street.'

'If not,' she said seriously, 'my life's been without point.'

'*That* makes you sound like a lot of others.'

'I don't mind sounding like them, just being like them.'

'Well, where have I seen you?'

'I've been on the programme a few times. I'm not much of a performer, but he uses me for class golks. And then I started as you did, a victim. In Delman's. I was buying shoes. Golk was the salesman. He kept bringing the wrong size and trying to cram me into them. I was just about to kick his teeth out. He stopped just in time.' The last came out with a kind of bemused nostalgia.

'I saw it. I'm sure. I remember it. Mostly your face.'

'Don't tell that to Golk.'

'Why not? Doesn't he want to make the amateur, the man in the street, memorable?'

'I told you you'll have to let him tell you what he wants. I don't know and don't much care. And anyway, Golk didn't make me memorable, I made one of his golks memorable, and that I don't think he wants. And don't compliment me; it sticks in my gut. Just relax.'

Hondorp shoved the mussels across the table. 'All right. Fine. I get you.'

Hendricks put her hand on his. 'Look,' she said with weary urgency. 'Be forgiving. I've got temperament up to here,' and she raised her hand to her throat and then dropped it back on his. 'And let's shake Golk for a while. When you come down to Parisak-land five or six days a

42

week, you begin to feel him around your neck like the albatross. It's too much.'

Hondorp thought of his father at the barometer. 'I suppose that's the way it is with jobs,' he said half to himself.

She shook her head. 'I think not,' she said, intrigued by the 'I suppose'. 'It's this job.'

'So what'll we do?' asked Hondorp, shifting gear.

The question hung in the air for a moment before Hendricks reluctantly took it out. 'There's not a damn thing to do in this city.'

'I wonder,' he said, smiling secretively and blushing a little. 'I confess to having spent quite a few happy hours here.'

'Doing what? The ball games? Movies? Shubert Alley? Carnegie Hall? The galleries? Shopping? Forest Hills? Blind Brook? The ferry? It's like a permanent World's Fair. Without the excitement of a temporary one. It's not a place. A place is somewhere you can manage. Where the variety is natural, not a series of spectaculars.'

'I haven't travelled,' said Hondorp. 'New York is most of what I know.'

She stared at him as if he were suffering a stroke. 'I don't know whether that's just the worst, or whether you're actually lucky. Would the devils have minded hell if they'd never known anything else?'

For the third time on the terrace, Hondorp had the sense of vista. This time there wasn't even an object to attach to it, nor did he possess any co-ordinates to locate it. Since he couldn't now credit what she'd said, he decided to discredit what she was. 'You're attitudinizing again. Like a bored *jeune fille* in Stendhal or the twenties.'

'I'm not a reader,' she said harshly. 'Don't confuse me with your tenth-rate little women.'

Hondorp, feeling his hook catch flesh, smiled coldly, and

said that he'd never do that. The meal finished out in a trance.

'Let's go,' she said, putting the apple core in his unfinished coffee cup. 'We're due to go on a golk at two-thirty.'

'I'm sorry about the *jeune fille.*'

'Not at all,' she said. 'I believe in applying what you read. Things are looking up now anyway. That's the strange thing: no matter how dull something is, it becomes tolerable when you golk it.'

The head waiter held the door for them. 'Good-bye, Mrs Hendricks,' he said, nodding fraternally to Hondorp.

III

For Hendricks, Hondorp constituted a diversion from a routine which, as she'd indicated to him, had come to smother her, and smother her in a fashion which made it nearly impossible for her to do anything about it, for even at its worst, it was incomparably more engaging than anything she'd ever done, indeed, anything she could now conceive of doing. And Hendricks had done a great deal, for although working for Golk was the only paid job she'd ever held, she'd come to it near the end of a long, brutal path.

She was the only child of two free-wheeling explosives of the jazz age, two conscious rioters who'd spent eight years assaulting each other with surprises until, finally, as the thirties took hold on them, Hendricks's mother delivered what turned out to be her final surprise, a baby whom she bore in a drunken haze and which helped kill her in the delivery room. At the funeral, Hendricks's father made drunken advances to an uncle's new wife, and this earned him a gaudy paragraph in two of the leading gossip columns

44

—now beginning to enjoy the powers of their spectacular malice on a national scale—and caused his monumentally indifferent family to take first notice and then steps. His mother, herself a savage, riotous dowager, who'd more or less retired from active combat with the Depression, took the infant to a winterized summer home in Watch Hill and let her grow up there under the barest tutelage of a foggy Irish couple until she was ready for boarding school. These fourteen marine years were, withal their increasing longueurs, the best Hendricks was to know.

At fifteen, she ran away from Miss Dobbs, running a Kotex pad up the flagpole as a mark of farewell. She'd earned more demerits for 'imperfection' than any girl who'd ever suffered Miss Dobbs's tutelage, and was consequently the feared idol of her contemporaries. The confidence this gave her failed at a matinée of *Carousel*, her second day on the loose; she gave herself meekly up to authority and was dispatched abroad to a boarding school at Vevey, the theory being that she could exercise less influence over foreigners and might therefore be subject to some.

She was. Her guide was a precocious Belgian lesbian, her room-mate a girl whose sexual hatred of men had turned philosophic and so helped forge independence. From her, or with her, Hendricks learned that she had a mind as well as a will, an open future rather than a timetable. Hendricks —then her name was Willoughby, Jeanine Willoughby— indulged the Belgian's raptures and received in turn the credo. She accepted all but the sexual article, and made her plans accordingly. It took her two years to get out of the school, years in which her chief pleasure was reading fiction, reading which, more than obliterating days, prepared her for more of the world than she would ever use. (And Hondorp had been right about Stendhal; she had found a prototype in Lamiel.)

At seventeen, she telegraphed her father that the school was a lesbian brothel and asked for money to travel with 'the family of a fellow-sufferer'. She gave the purported sufferer's surname as that of the American Ambassador to Belgium after determining from her room-mate that the Ambassador both had a family and one that was not likely to be known by anyone in her own. This precaution was taken more for her grandmother than her father. By the time the old woman learned the truth, Mr Willoughby had opened an account for Jeanine in Zürich and written the school to release her. She divided the account among six European banks and was off to Paris; if they were going to try and stop her, they were going to have a time of it. She wasn't stopped, and after a fruitless week, her grandmother stopped trying to stop her.

Her route was devious and brutal. It involved the common forms of unattached indulgence, the difference in Jeanine's case being that she was never at their mercy. She rationed her body as she did her money, and passed it out only for her own pleasure or to gain some other, limited end. She went through Europe assiduously, almost studiously, appraising her experience and discarding it after appraisal. This from her seventeenth to her nineteenth year.

One afternoon at the Hôtel Druot she had caught fire at three square inches of Goya etching and bid a quarter of a million francs which she didn't have for it. There had been a scene in the office during which Hendricks had exercised every seductive strategy she'd mastered in the last two years with absolutely no visible effect on the sleek official whose eye went over her as if she were a shabby, unsellable *objet d'art*. It was not the first time that her eight thousand dollars a year had seemed to her little more than a trap for her desires, enough money to let her view pleasures she could not afford. The pleasures the money did allow her seemed to her only the most ordinary or most bizarre. For a few months she tried speculating on the Bourse and then, via her father, in the commodity markets. The gambit forced her to touch capital. Then she bought a surplus army plane, sold it for a small paint factory in Meudon-Val-Fleury, and sold that for a shipment of Italian typewriters which were hijacked outside of Vicenza.

After this collapse, she decided to marry, to marry money, and Immanuel Kant's glacial definition of marriage became her guide, her image of the woman-crippling condition. Marriage to money meant a return to the United States: European wealth was too remote and the techniques of entrapment too involved for a single girl, no matter how *beyliste*. So she came back, first to Watch Hill, then to New York where she made a swift and useless pass at a début, moved on to Sea Island, Prout's Neck, Newport, Hobe Sound, Pasadena, the West Indies, and then, her gorge stuffed with the inane vulgarities of courtship, returned to Paris, met George Hendricks at a party in the Longchamps enclosure, and married him. Her life later seemed to her to have been but preparation for this terrible error.

George Hendricks was the son of a Soho whore and a Manchester assurance man. He was also the son-in-law of Laomedon Demicapoulos, one of the great Hellenic free-booters who had swept up the usable debris of the Second World War and emerged as not only a billionaire but almost as an independent nation. Hendricks was a brilliant time-server, an accounting wizard with a flare for violence. By the time he married Demicapoulos's daughter, he had three million dollars of his own and controlled eighty times that amount. Six years later he was said to be worth sixty million. Prising him free from the Greek's only daughter was for Jeanine a labour that seemed to her worthy of her training.

When it was all over, it turned out that her machinations

and chicanery were the objects of her husband's and his first wife's entertainment. Neither of them had been interested in the other since the first month of their marriage. Jeanine's difficulties and stratagems provided them with the only really pleasurable fruit of it.

Jeanine's marriage was her rack. Hendricks's contempt and detestation were unbounded in extent and savagery, and she was for him little more than a laboratory in which he experimented with the odder aspects of his passions. He moved systematically to grind down every gesture of the independence whose existence represented the creative act of Jeanine's life. Far beyond her in strength and shrewdness, his typical strategy was to rouse an argument, and lead it on and on until he'd led her to see herself self-contradicted, exposed, ridiculous. He baited her to rage, and fed it until it became violence; then he counterpunched her attacks, knocked her groggy, threw her into bed or on the floor, and then, often as not, assaulted her.

It went on like this for nine months. She had held on thinking that sheer holding on would break him. When she'd made better gauge of his tenacity, she ran off, half-dead, to Brussels where her old room-mate took her in and introduced her to a narcotic bliss which saved her sanity.

For fifteen months she lived in haze. She came to one day after a fall down the stone steps in the Jardins Royales, came to to find herself prominent and bloody. That very night, bandaged and aching, she lit out for Bad Gastein— she'd been reading a book on mad King Ludwig—and there she locked herself in a hotel room and fought the cramping pains of privation. 'My labour pains,' she said, gripping the headboard, huddling under quilts, ripping the sheets, 'and I come out my own child.'

And she did, feeble, tearful, unco-ordinated, then took the Kur and came slowly back to strength and self-control.

She sailed to America, went out to Nevada and sued Hendricks for divorce. In return for its being uncontested —and she well knew what a contest there could have been with him, even in Nevada—she received nothing from him but—a gesture she did not bother to fathom—an International Air Travel and Diner's Club Card, a two-thousand-dollar insurance policy on his life taken out especially for the occasion, and a letter entitling her to distinguished consideration from all agents of the Demicapoulos concerns. She accepted these along with the divorce and went back to New York, took a room at the Ambassador and began to look for a way to come all the way to life.

She was twenty-two, and on the edge of change, either of something outside the world of what she thought of as 'experience for its own sake' or, if necessary, of that politic female submission she had long ago fought to a standstill.

And then, two months after her return, while she was in Delman's buying shoes, she was golked.

When the salesman pulled the red beard off his chin, Hendricks burst into a laughter to which her vocal cords were so unused that they ached for minutes after, and when half an hour later in the Sherry Netherlands Bar, Golk invited her to join his crew, she laughed again, laughed for minutes until Golk saw that there was more relief than amusement in it. That night they went out to dinner, and by that time she had accepted more than the original invitation.

The other invitation was hedged by commentary. 'I'm either incapable of or powerfully unwilling to enter a long-drawn-out relationship,' Golk said in the elaborate, deadly manner which was the one he employed for extra-studio situations. He said it as they ate dessert, and showed her with half-smile and open hand that for him the importance of such a relationship could be measured by that brief, sweet course. Then, as was his custom also, he said what he had just been at pains to explain without saying, namely that in this respect he was continental. 'And,' he went on, 'as with Europeans, dessert is not the end of my meals.'

If the invitation was hedged, it wasn't brutal, and for Hendricks, that meant a great deal. 'I've always thought', he said with that rare sweetness which always seemed unexpected to her, the amazing return on a forgotten sweepstake ticket, 'that the basis for the whole thing was —is—part of legitimate curiosity, for the wisdom that nothing else supplies. It's got nothing to do with experience, and nothing serious to do with natural urges. Good men have lived without it. If I don't pick up something besides a quick boot or a whiff of hashish every time, it's as if I haven't done it.'

Hendricks, to whom the countless variations of the countless approaches to this imperial city were rutted with familiarity, found this hodgepodge somehow touching.

He went on. 'When love gets to be important to someone, it means that he hasn't been able to manage something else. Falling in love seems to me an almost sure sign of failure. Except for the very few who have a real talent for it. I grant that. Of course, it's a minor talent. Though that may be too hasty. Who's to judge what's minor? To the *Atlantic Monthly*, I'm minor. In fact, I'm nowhere.'

Golk's notions about love did not, in Hendricks's authoritative view, drastically affect his practice. At least, he neither enlarged nor soured the range of her experience. She enjoyed being with him, making love or not, and she was with him too seldom to fall into that nauseating satiety everything brought her so much more quickly than she thought just.

It was about the time when she began to look forward to evenings with him, suspensefully, even fearfully, that he abandoned her, called her but once a month and then usually at two or three o'clock on rainy mornings asking her to hoof it over to his apartment. She always did, happier in being the therapy for his cauchemars than in being anyone else's daydream. The calls apparently came after he hadn't been able to figure something or other out, a particular golk, or some notion he wanted to write out in his journal. He always told her this as an apology for his request; it made little difference to her by this time.

When Hondorp joined the golks, she hadn't been called in five months, and her memory of the nocturnal pleasure reposed with most of her life in the oblivion she contrived for it.

Oblivion had about undone all but one night with him, a night which escaped not because of its intrinsic pleasure, but because it puzzled her understanding of him. It had begun with an unusual golk, the victim of which was a Lower East Side Italian mother of eleven children who would not react to the frustrations which were to form the centre of the scene, but instead took the rebuffs with a dignified, tolerant, intelligent humour which made the golk successful despite the lack of the dramatic centre Golk was working for. Golk had played the part of an itinerant fruit and vegetable pedlar selling his goods at suspiciously low prices. Another victim, also Italian, raucous, expressive, a natural comic, had risen to the bait, let her suspicions grow until the fruit which would reveal no flaw to her rigorous search was damned and refused on the grounds that 'it was-a *too* good'. The second woman Golk could not excite; sudden shifts in the position of apples, looks of leering triumph as she made a purchase, lowering the price of refused items still more, offering to give them away, nothing shook the easy achievement of her mission. Failing here, Golk started talking to the woman about her family, baiting her gently about their number, her cooking, and then, suddenly, he was invited to dinner that night, and accepted. And he went, with Hendricks, Fitch, and the camera.

It was a vinous, pasty orgy. Bowls of spaghetti darkened by islands of onion, spiced meat, and peppers were emptied within seconds of being put on the table. Bottles of raw, amber Brindisi gurgled down fifteen throats. Golk, at the table, hurled great gobs of food into his mouth, raced the others to refills, burped monstrously, looked glazed, talked a kind of pidgin Italian, and then flopped on a couch and snored while the family circled him laughing. Fitch let the camera grind on, 'cranking it' only when he ran out of film.

The next day, Klebba objected strenuously to the footage. 'It's pointless,' he said. 'A bunch of lousy hogs. And you don't seem planted there,' he said to Golk. 'Just another hoggish wop. What's the point?'

'We'll use it,' Golk said. 'It's one of the greatest golks I've ever made.' And he had it shown again and would permit no cuts. It would be shown in two parts on the programme.

'Like Stroheim making *Greed*,' said Klebba. 'Just put in every damn thing the camera can see. No quality, just footage.'

Golk looked at it again. 'An uncomic wopera,' was his description of it, and the phrase allayed all complaints from the golks.

By the next night, they had persuaded him to cut it down to one full programme, and after they'd done the editing, he and Hendricks went out to dinner, and that night she told him the story of her marriage, the only part of her life that he hadn't heard or asked her about.

They walked up Fifth Avenue in the cold November night, and in the frosty light angling up from the pavements, Golk glowed blue like a Christmas tree bulb. Their furred arms—Golk wore a racoon coat, Hendricks a mink—were linked at the elbows.

'Once we were at Longchamps,' she began.

'What's that?' He knew who 'we' meant.

'A race track in the Bois de Boulogne. In Paris. We were out there, and I was having what was for me a pretty good day, one winner across the board out of five races. In the sixth I had a hunch, a genuine hunch. You know, you feel chill on your skin.'

'Yes.'

'It was a filly named Zut Alors. I gave George all I had around, about four hundred thousand francs, and told him to bet it win and show. Occasionally he'd do errands like that with a sort of blank coldness that was supposed to make you say, "Never mind, I'll do it myself". But I was used to him. Know what he did?'

Golk shook his head; the question was just for taking sight on the outrage.

'The horse belonged to some French banker. George didn't know him from Adam, but he went into the club-house, found the fellow, and right then and there, *sur le champ* as they say, he bought the horse using my four hundred thousand as first payment. I think Demicapoulos had some hold on the guy. Or maybe not. George had great powers of persuasion. Anyway he went down with this fellow, got the jockey as he was mounting for the race, took him aside and told him to come in no better than fourth. Then he came back and told me what he'd done. The whole thing didn't take more than twenty or twenty-five minutes, just the time between races. You know what he said?' Golk shook his head. 'He said, "It'll teach you the inadvisability of playing hunches. Only certain people can play hunches. Those who don't have to." What do you think of that?'

Golk said nothing.

'He used to hire cars to follow me when I was driving somewhere. I'd be going out to Versailles, or just going to shop, and all of a sudden there'd be a smack on my bumper. I knew what was what. I'd give it a run, but half the time this damn thing would be bumping me, just bumping me. I'd try to manœuvre where there'd be a *flic*——'

'A cop?'

'Yes. But he'd have scooted. And then pick me up again. I gave up driving.'

They had reached the Plaza and walked around to the Park side and gone into the Oak Bar. There was almost no one else there, and Hendricks, who kept on talking even as Golk ordered, seemed a kind of fortune teller sitting in the dark, extravagant room with the snow mural, telling her past as if it were the dread future of an insensitive client. After another half-hour's worth of talk, she stopped, less because she'd run out of brutalities than because she became more aware of Golk's cool, unmoved study of them. Yet stopping, she felt the strangeness of his large, warm palm on her hand, felt it abstractly stroking, reassembling as it were what his eye was breaking down. His look had been like a well-shaft thrust into her body, and she had felt herself yielding what counted for her as she'd never before yielded even to herself. Now, hand to hand, she felt not restoration of what she'd yielded, but the peace of having made some sense out of what had been little more than pain, fury, unreason.

After a while, he said, 'You know, some of that divorce settlement might come in handy.'

'I've never used it. If I were starving, I don't know if I'd use his lousy Diner's Card.'

'Let's use it tonight,' he said.

'All right,' she said easily.

'I can even use that letter to old Demicapoulos.'

54

'It's to his agents,' she said. 'And what do you think you can do with the goddam thing?'

'There's almost nothing in this world that I can't find a use for,' he said without smiling.

'Yes,' she said, before suppressing any egoistic reference from the reply, 'I'm aware of that. I'll bring you the letter.'

'Let's go,' he said, and he called the waiter, wrote down the Diner's Card number and signed her name. They got their coats and went out the north exit into the cold wind blowing down Central Park South. They crossed over to the Park side, and, in the dark, Golk took her head in his hand and, as if testing a new wine, delicately, knowledgeably kissed her.

'Oh,' she said, after this. 'Oh, oh, oh.'

'You know,' he said, 'it's a strange race that can claim you and that damn wop woman as parts of one species.' He took her arm and they walked back to his apartment, a long, cold walk which tired them only near the very end. They walked close together, the fur coats blending so they seemed the hide of one immense animal.

It was the closest she had been to Golk, but the next day, coming to work—she had gone home to change in the meantime—she found in him no mark of their intimacy. The night had taken what it had supplied. And there were no more such nights.

IV

Every clear day from the end of March to the beginning of December, the chess and checker players assembled at the table-benches put up for them by the Department of Parks in a grassy enclosure in uptown Central Park, a few hundred yards west of the public tennis courts and somewhat farther north of a kiddies' playground. The chess and checker players were almost entirely men over sixty-five, although there were a few younger men, petty *rentiers* or pensioned invalids, and an even fewer number of old women; the latter showed up mostly on warmer days. The regulars were a coat-and-tie crowd; informality was frowned upon unless there was medical justification for it, although in the winter, the unspoken rules permitted a great variety of hats, astrakhans, berets, caps of all sorts, winter Alpines, scarves of many colours, lengths, and textures, and heavy overcoats, usually battered and bearing the marks of ones which would not be replaced.

In the warm months, along with the return of the women regulars, there were frequent stragglers, mostly fresh kids either to be ignored or bounced out by the Park Department's attendant, tennis players coming back from the courts, or simply passers-by intrigued by the sight of forty or fifty grey heads bent over the long green tables. Occasionally stragglers found out that for a quarter the attendant would give them a board and men. (The regulars paid two dollars a year for a licence entitling them to unlimited use of the facilities.) Sometimes seven or eight stragglers' games went on at once which meant that a few regulars were temporarily displaced. Temporarily, because only the hardiest or dullest interlopers could withstand the expelling stares of the regulars. Stragglers were tolerated if they watched quietly—like the ten steady kibitzers of the group—or if they filled in as the opponent of a regular temporarily without a game and acted as if they knew they were being granted a courtesy. Most of the regulars were chess players only; the checker players were looked down upon, and occupied the peripheral tables, a fragile shell around the kernel of the chess players.

On a fine blue April day, the regulars were out in force.

There was a stragglers' game going on as well, one which was attracting an inordinate amount of attention. Players and kibitzers diverted glances from their own positions to the solution of the bizarre couple playing in the unfavourable north-east corner of the enclosure. The couple consisted of a short, well-dressed man wearing a black Homburg out of which sluiced effusions of red hair and a young Negress in a remarkably bulging black sheath. By her side was a large suitcase, which constituted for the regulars one of the major mysteries about the pair. 'Could be she's got no place to go,' said one of the most distinguished regulars, Frankl. His opponent, Heinemann, a little man who curved around himself like a snarl of grey wool, depressed his head even farther than usual between his shoulders and then stretched the muscles of his lower jaw to complete the Eastern European shrug of 'Could be'.

It was not customary for stragglers' games to attract even straggling kibitzers, but three strange men and a woman were watching this game. One of the men, dressed in workman's clothes, was carrying an oddly protuberant lunch box which he shifted carefully at intervals, as if there were a sick animal inside it. 'Maybe likes fresh meat for dinner,' was Frankl's whispered explanation of this phenomenon. Heinemann supplied the shrug and then blinked with fright as he noticed the lunch box shift menacingly towards him. 'A tommy-gun,' was his shattering unexpressed notion. He sat paralysed till the black muzzle moved away from him.

The stragglers had come up separately, yet they seemed to cohere like a retinue. Occasionally they bent down to murmur something to the man, and once one of them bent towards the woman's suitcase and actually touched it, although for what purpose no regular's eyesight was good enough to determine.

All of a sudden the woman cried out, 'What do you think you're doing with that knight, man?'

Every regular's eye in the enclosure bent towards the outburst.

The Homburg's boisterous response was, 'Get your cotton-picking hands off that piece.'

'What do you think there, man, that's a rook and bishop all in one?' answered the Sheath, her hand pushing the piece one way while the Homburg pushed it another. 'And if you want to try Indian wrestling,' she went on, 'I'll throw you half-way across the park.'

'*Sag' ihm was*, Julius,' whispered Heinemann to Frankl, his imagination opening on to a scene of violence which he knew would end his days there and then on the enclosure grounds.

Frankl, the man whose custom it was to say 'shah mat', 'the king is dead', instead of 'checkmate', whose scholarly authority was solicited for all refined judgements among the regulars, who had in private life, twenty-five years before, been a not-unsuccessful petty manufacturer of dress goods, Frankl rose to the perils of the occasion, stood up and went over to the disputants. 'May I be of some assistance?' he asked in a voice which all of his authority could not keep unwavering.

'Are you a chess player?' asked the man in the Homburg, giving Frankl a blue look which seemed to call in question the necessity of old men.

The response of the regulars to this inquiry was divided between a feverish incomprehension and suffocated hysteria. Above their mutters, Heinemann's 'Ha, ha, ha' wavered like a blown flag.

'I happen to be,' said Frankl with a modest dignity that stiffened the regulars with admiration. 'Indeed,' he continued in a more expansive and natural manner, 'some of my friends consider me an authority of sorts.' He took from an inside pocket a squat, dirty tome, *Rehboch and the Viennese Middle Game*, displayed it, and said, 'You see, I am a reader as well as a participant.'

'Excellent,' said the Homburg.

'You said it,' came from the Sheath. 'Now look here at this move he's trying to make with his knight here. And you know what he tells me?'

'What?' asked Frankl, watching with amazement as a dark finger moved the knight from King 3 to Queen 8.

'I told her,' interrupted the Homburg, his eye flashing with what even Frankl could now see was mania, 'that in the Goldsmith-Benjamino gambit, the knight has the option of doubling and reversing its move, something that I did not expect to have to tell anyone who has played, or claims to have played'— and here he fixed his grinding eye on his opponent's face—'the royal game.'

'Hm,' said Frankl, and he made a half-turn towards his expectant fellows.

'You admit you'd castled, don't you?' pursued the Homburg.

'I brushed my teeth this morning too,' responded the girl. 'What's that got to do with the price of baked beans?'

'Bravo,' muttered Heinemann. 'An intelligent floozie.'

'Quiet,' said Frankl, now bent over the board. After a minute of reflection, and a few seconds of inadequate attempts to straighten up, he came erect, discharged an immense wad of spittle into the bushes, and said, 'Foul play.'

'What's that?' demanded the Homburg, his eyes glittering.

Frankl, clutching his book, braved the madness. 'Listen, mister,' he said. 'Since 1880, sixty-five years almost, I'm playing chess. In that time, in my entire career, playing, reading, talking, not one word have I heard about Gold-smith-Benjamino. One word? Not one syllable.' He planted a tiny fist into a receptive little palm and turned to Heinemann for verification and relief.

'*Unerhört*,' said Heinemann quietly.

'You see, mister,' said Frankl sweetly. 'That's my reason for saying "Foul play".'

The man in the Homburg wiped his head with a great handkerchief, looked around wildly at the accumulating circle of regulars, and said, 'Is there no one here in this famous group of chess and checker players of whom all New York knows, is there no one here who can enlighten these frazzleheads about the famous convention which I employed, and which my father learned directly from Gold-smith himself?'

The inimical silence was broken into by a tiny old woman regular, Miss Morseburger, who came up to the Homburg, shook his hand, and said in a loud baritone, 'I can enlighten. I'm Morseburger. My brother, Jules Ferry Morseburger, for many years second board of the Respighi Club, employed the convention of which you speak not once, not twice, but innumerable and frequent times.'

Heinemann made a series of small circles with his hand. 'Notorious,' he said. '*Ganz verrückt.*'

'With due respect,' said Frankl, his little white head dark with rebuke, 'Miss Morseburger is, I think, confusing the alleged convention with an established one. I think our job here is ended.'

He started to turn back but was halted by a scream. It was Miss Morseburger. 'Look,' she cried, pointing to the man with the Homburg who was not only removing *it*, but removing the mop of red hair beneath it, abandoning an immense, hairless skull to the sun.

'It's that Golk,' shrieked Miss Morseburger.

V

'There are two pivots to the golks we're doing these days,' said Golk from the driver's seat to Hondorp who sat with Fitch, Benson, and Elaine in the back of the station wagon. They were driving up to Central Park. 'The hook in the worm is one. You dangle a prize before a victim, play him like a hooked carp, and while he watches, turn the prize to dust.' Hondorp, who had recently seen a smallish prize dangled before him and then turn to dust, was not offended by the awkwardness of the figure. 'That's how we played that old Whiskers yesterday with the Shakespeare. The other kind is the kind we played on you. Stepping in between a man and his legitimate pleasures. We thwart a man from the satisfaction of the appetites he's entitled to.'

'One isn't entitled to appetites,' said Hendricks in those waspish tones in which Hondorp had discerned the note of true style during lunch. She was sitting flank to flank with Golk in the front seat. 'One has them. You talk about managing people. You can't even manage an English sentence.'

Golk hesitated over her reprimand but didn't let it affect the instruction he was giving Hondorp. 'Like a few weeks ago. We were golking in a Whelan's up on Broadway. I was jerking sodas behind the counter. Klebba was a decoy customer. A guy would come in and order a sundae, say, and I'd take a long time getting it to him, and when I did, it was a cherry frappé. There'd be a fuss, and I'd ask Klebba if the guy hadn't ordered a cherry frappé. He'd say, "Yes", and we were off. A couple of them admitted they were wrong. Some little guy flung a glass of water at me. It was a very successful operation. Right?'

'Right,' said Fitch.

'Thwarted appetite. That was the pivot. Now we're going to work a variation of it. These whiskers up here play chess two hundred days a year, morning, noon, and night. The only thing that stops them is the undertaker. Well, we're the undertakers today. Get it?'

'Yes,' said Hondorp. 'I follow you.'

'The principle isn't complicated. A principle better not be. But on camera, you're on the highwire. Almost like live TV, though they're always working from a script, or at such low tension it doesn't matter, or from the news event which is mostly out of their hands, but you make a mistake on this show, and you've ruined a good idea, an afternoon, and a lot of film. You don't repeat golks. Like lightning. Get it?'

'Yes,' said Hondorp. 'I get it.'

In the rear-view mirror, Hendricks studied Hondorp. Ever since the head waiter had said, 'Good-bye, Mrs Hendricks,' he had been a study in discomfort, one which she had had no thought of provoking, but which she relished. 'A natural victim,' was her assessment of him, for within the limits of Hondorp's impassivity she could read the flickers of distress, pleasure, and now, as he listened to Golk's lecture, melancholy boredom on his dark face. It was what she thought of an an 'amateur's face', a map on which exploiters could trace with ease their devious routes. It was not her own ambition to exploit it. If anything, it was to harden the face, or rather, harden the man behind it so that the signs of pleasure and distress would be blurred into a worldly neutrality. This was, she felt, what lay in the back of Golk's injunction to 'whip him into shape'. 'It's not just showing him the ropes. Golk wants something basic,' was her thought.

They entered the Park at Seventy-second and drove the sweeping curves up to a clearing at Ninety-first. They parked and made preparations: Golk put on his wig and Homburg, Elaine a swash of lipstick and some junk jewellery, Fitch adjusted the camera in the odd lunch box, and Benson manipulated the complex innards of the suitcase.

'Elaine and I first,' said Golk. 'Then Benson with the suitcase. Billy, you wait five minutes with the camera; Hondorp, you five more, and Hendricks five more. Remember to keep the lunch box clear.' He crooked his arm; Elaine took it and they sauntered off to the enclosure, a few hundred yards away.

'Cute couple,' said Fitch, his ship's head pointed for breeze.

'They should be,' said Hendricks.

'Women,' said Benson and moved off.

'Nervous?' Hendricks asked Hondorp when they were waiting by themselves.

'What from?'

'I don't know. You seem a little withdrawn.'

'Just thinking,' he said, trying to be neither snappish nor relaxed. 'There's been a lot to think about today.'

'If you have any questions about anything, don't be afraid to ask me,' she said.

'When I've accumulated a few, I'll put them to you all at once.' Hondorp had had little experience of being led on by the beak, but he knew when it was happening what to do about it. The pique which had set this off, the annoyance at the disparity between Hendricks's easy manner, ringless finger, and his present ignorance of her status—widow, divorcee, faker, mother of five—which the head waiter's farewell had forced on him, this annoyance he was unwilling to ask about, but eager to forget. Identifying its source, Hendricks found it both too trifling and too titillating to bother about.

'You go on up now,' she said, a whip of command in her voice.

'Another twist of the screw,' he thought. 'All right. I'm with her,' and aloud, 'Is there any way you might suggest that I walk up there?'

'Try to hold your butt in a little. I think it's that genteel stoop of yours that pushes it out.'

A patronizing, indulging-the-nasty-nephew turn of his lips countered this. 'I've got her when she starts that,' he thought.

And correctly. Hendricks, watching him stroll off, his stoop perceptibly greater, his backside aimed at her, felt the rare twinge of a strategic error. 'Not such a pushover after all,' she thought, loping slowly after him now, and smiling with even more than the anticipation she normally felt at the shooting of a golk.

VI

At the revelation that they were On Camera, that the breach of the enclosure's peace had been staged, that the fire didn't burn, there was a pandemonium of shy joy. All the regulars but Miss Morseburger crowded around Golk and the golks, shaking their hands, congratulating them, asking when the programme would be telecast. Fitch passed out release slips, and these were signed with the authoritative flourishings of constitutional delegates. At one suggestion that the Goldsmith-Benjamino convention was not without a certain technical interest, there was restrained rather than jeering laughter. 'Perhaps so,' said Frankl generously. And this remark so restored equilibrium to the enclosure that even Miss Morseburger came forward to shake Golk's hand, if briefly and sadly.

The old people's excitement roused a corresponding excitement in Hondorp, though one which permitted him to distinguish his from theirs. His own was that of an Olympian watching himself being recognized by mortals after the execution of an unearthly feat. He beamed as if from a cloud as Elaine autographed Frankl's copy of *Rehboch and the Viennese Middle Game.*

'I shall treasure it all my life,' said the little octogenarian. Elaine kissed his grey poll and said that she hoped that would be for some time then.

'They sure are cute,' she said to Hondorp, squeezing his arm for emphasis.

Hondorp's excitement was readily convertible. Indeed the whole day had been marked for him by this ready convertibility, as if one knowledge refused to come unless refuelled by others. His eye coursed Elaine's spectacular shape with that sense of large exploration which had been the key signature of his day.

'Let's you and me go out a little after,' she said with the animal tact that spared him the effort of working up to a similar proposal. He sighed with relief and nodded.

Hendricks, who had watched them with angry amusement, told herself it was just as well that Hondorp get over 'that stage'. 'She can take the kinks out, and it'll give him some assurance. Primitive, but, I suppose, necessary.'

She went over to Golk and translated this into action. 'Why don't you let Hondorp off the hook for today? He can go off and relax with the nigger. He's had about as much of your crap as a sane man can take in a day.'

Golk was bidding the chess players elaborate farewells, but sandwiched in his consent. 'All right,' and he called over to Hondorp. 'You can go on now. You too, Elaine. We'll show you the results tomorrow.' And he patted old

Heinemann on the backside and said that some day he would enjoy playing a real game with him.

'What results?' Hondorp asked Elaine as they walked off.

'You know,' she said. 'This golk we just shot here. What results were you thinking of?'

'I just don't know,' he said, knowing of course that the confusion of the two distinct programmes of action which had been thrown down to him today was something he was not going to work out with ease or speed.

'I'm going to straighten you all out, honey,' she said in that manner which was, as he saw it, its own caricature. 'We'll pump a little booze into you and then we'll be able to pump all the other troubles out.'

Too much, thought Hondorp. Life wasn't built along such straight tracks. He suspected in Elaine a more elliptical route, and the suspicion was enough to clear the way, where more of the sheer, overt movement would have clotted in him the desire which had edged his day and which needed, he knew, to be planed off.

They went to the Penny Bar. 'One of the few stills that supplies Pernod in this town,' said Elaine. 'And I got a penchant for things French. Just like the frogs have for me and mine.' She put one of her legs around his under the table. 'I knew you had plenty of life in you,' she added, feeling him tighten up.

They drank for an hour, enough to free Hondorp from any remaining clot, yet not enough to free him from anything else. The other reason for coming to the bar was now unveiled to him: Elaine lived in the hotel above it. He was but eight floors away from the end of that desire whose fangs had bitten into him this morning. He could barely contain himself in the elevator.

They rushed down the hall to her room, started stripping

at the door and fell on the bed. Hondorp reeled with an explosion of pleasure.

After the ecstatic fall-out, they dragged their organs apart and lay, legs intertwined, breathing hard. 'That myth about you Africans is true,' gasped Hondorp.

Elaine laughed with fury. 'That's me, not Africa,' she said, 'just me,' and she rolled over on him to extract another groan of weary pleasure. That what she supplied was so freely given and so inexhaustibly there, fattened Hondorp's own supply. 'You're like the white man's dream of it,' he managed after their next engagement.

'That's my aim in life,' she said. 'I never sleep with a jig.'

'Golk ought to get you on film.'

'Oh, Hondorp-lover,' she said, draping over him and wriggling to squeeze out the tube's last drop. 'Golkie had me on film the second night. He shows it to the sponsors.'

'What a man is our Golk,' muttered Hondorp, on the edge of sleep. He dropped off then, with a last, half-conscious glimpse of Elaine somehow all over him trying to coax another flicker from his alien, depleted flesh.

CHAPTER THREE

I

HONDORP went down to the Parisak Building every day but Sunday. 'We work constantly but easily,' said Golk. 'Just turn up an hour or so before lunch. That way, some of that salivation is going to work for us, yet you won't get knocked out by your first stint.'

'A strange schedule,' said Poppa Hondorp to himself as he left his son at the breakfast table still in bathrobe and pyjamas. 'Some uniform for a business man.' Now that Hondorp was a man of affairs, he luxuriated in the signs of idleness which before had shamed him. For Poppa Hondorp, business was business, and lousy as it was, it meant no pyjamas at eight-thirty in the morning. The outfit was just one of the many alterations in their relationship which he had already accustomed himself not to talk about. After the initial shock, the minor alterations were, in fact, almost welcome.

That first night, when his son had not come home until three in the morning, and worse, not telephoned warning of the impending defection, had caused the household to sway on its foundations. Dinner had been postponed until eight o'clock; Poppa Hondorp had missed Groucho and Broken Arrow (or Dragnet—he alternated) and had waited up four and a half hours later than his usual bedtime. His son had found him snoring in front of the blank, humming TV screen.

'You still up, Poppa?' he asked with some fright and much surprise.

Poppa Hondorp had staggered up from a dream to his

son's questioning face, and then held out his arms as if to embrace him. Whether he'd changed his mind in mid-air or not, Hondorp did not know; he did know that he'd been simultaneously whacked on both cheeks, and that the whacks had been followed by what proved to be one of Poppa's last 'old-style' pronouncements, 'No son of mine is coming into the home at four o'clock in the morning.' While Hondorp hesitated about whether to correct the hour, his father had burst into tears, kissed the cheeks where he'd slapped them, and waddled off down the hall to his bedroom.

Since that time, Poppa Hondorp had reacted to the injuries his son inflicted with first theatrical, then actual stoicism, while his son tried to alleviate the pain by telephoning about any derangement his plans might work in the household.

But the suppression of what he was accustomed to give easy vent to wrought internal changes in Poppa Hondorp. A lipoma began forming at the base of his neck, and with corporal sympathy his varicose veins twitched and swelled. Poppa's own diagnosis of the neck ornament was 'fatty deposit due to circulatory impairment caused by subvention of some parasitic organism', but he did not venture beyond diagnosis to therapy. Indeed, he seemed to relish this bodily version of his family situation: 'I cease playing host to my son and receive in his place a worm.'

'You ought to let Frankhauser look over you, Poppa,' was his son's advice. (Frankhauser was a general diagnostician with whom Poppa Hondorp exchanged services.)

'No Frankhauser can bring me to health, darling. You know what ails me,' and the old man unleashed—in the theatrical mode—his immense version of a sigh, and toppled a half-inch of cigar ash into his coffee. He tipped the contents into his throat, shivered with melancholy pleasure, kissed his son on the cheek, called good-bye to the cook, and limped—another concession to the theatre—out of the room and front door.

The breakfast exchanges, once the tensest of Hondorp's days, were now but gentle prologues to them. Caught up in Golk's fierce tide, Hondorp's head swarmed with the novel procedures of editing, mixing, blooping, trimming, cutting, scouting, the special routines which composed the operation of making golks. Since all of Golk's people were more or less transposable parts of his machine, all capable of doing a little bit of almost everything, Hondorp's first weeks existed for him as a great storm of facts. That which gave it coherence was the great fact that there was a storm and that he was the object, or chief barometer of it. For him, the storm became more and more Golk, the aspect of Golk in action, and the ubiquity and ever-moving knowingness which this meant became for him, even before he was conscious that he'd abandoned his amused, even faintly contemptuous admiration for Golk, a kind of credo. If in the midst of some blood-letting job he found on him Golk's grin or wink or pat, storm turned to light and warmth, and the reason for all the blood became clear.

The new knowledge was not only technical; indeed, as Hendricks told him, the technical part was mere packaging. One of the pleasantest of the other parts was 'scouting'. Two or three afternoons a week, golks would go out together around the city, sometimes with cameras, sometimes not. They walked or drove, and as far as direction went, it was in the haphazard one that Hondorp had followed for years by himself. In no other way was it haphazard: they were doing reconnaissance work for future golks, and every glance was a study heavy with consequence. Each store, each street, each potential situation had to be assessed in terms of space for equipment, possibility of crippling disturbances, light, noise, the numerous pre-requisites for usable golks. Scouting was neither relaxing nor exciting, but it was never boring; at the end of an afternoon of it, Hondorp would go home and sleep.

He usually went out on the expeditions with Hendricks. Golk liked to see them together. 'You set each other off,' was his appraisal of their tandem appearances. 'You're both kind of sour, but Hendricks is light sour, Hondorp dark sour.'

Under the pressures of association, Hondorp's uneasy ignorance of Hendricks's status gave way to a peculiar intimacy. They first exchanged cryptic but informative references to their respective histories, and this led them to equality, if not yet companionship. Hendricks had begun the exchange, begun it purposely and carefully. Her old desire to keep what surrounded her on permanent alert was almost entirely gone. Not even the prospect of the comparatively easy victory she still saw in Hondorp drew her back to the battlefields where her independence had been shaped. The dark oddball, Hondorp, seemed to her a not unpleasant adjunct to a good many hours, a part of the soft turf on which she had luckily landed after being tossed over the cliff by George Hendricks.

The occasions when they went out by themselves were, for both of them, preferable to the ones in which Golk joined them. In Hondorp's third week, Golk had turned melancholy, or, at least, darkly thoughtful. And though he claimed to enjoy being with them, he communicated to them largely by issuing orders, or by snapped correction of their judgements. One day, after the three of them had shot some exploratory footage in a Second Avenue bar, Hendricks spelled out her interpretation of the mood for Hondorp. Golk himself had gone back to the studio, and she and Hondorp sat at the counter of a hamburger joint.

Below the level of the counter, Hondorp wiped his spoon on a paper napkin, and asked her, 'Well, what is wrong with him?'

'Ambition,' she said bitterly. 'He's getting ready to unload.'

'That's splendid. Why the I-smell-shit look?'

'I'll tell you,' she said, and bit into the flavoured lard of a doughnut while she thought how to tell him. For him, her head had taken on in the joint's fluorescents a kind of vaporous gold which shook him as she hadn't shaken him before. It was the vapour of inimitable gentility and prevailed against the gabardine slacks she wore and the dull crockery and rank doughnuts which, against her lips, seemed the gross world's foul attempt to fuel the fine spirit. 'It's like Saturn,' she said. 'Now we're independent moons, or at least identifiable ones, stuck fast as we are. From what he's planning now, we're going to be one undifferentiated, subservient ring, just something to set him off.'

For Hondorp, the vapour became annoying, a female fog. 'Nonsense.'

'What little identity we have now, he's going to cut us loose from, every scrap of it.'

'So what?' said Hondorp, and he slurped his coffee to accentuate the belligerence this suffragette protest roused in him. Speculation about motives or about the future was not his cup of tea, and female investment in such speculation stirred his rage. 'What do we have to do that's better, whether we're partners or serfs?' Hendricks's face drew into battle formation, as he went on. 'And who're you to cast your great analytic powers on what your betters are doing?'

Hendricks slammed a fifty-cent piece on the counter, and didn't wait for change. Hondorp's belligerence vanished. He put down a dime and followed her. They didn't talk, but moved up Second Avenue at a clip which the sun soon reduced to a breathless amble. It reduced the force of anger and belligerence as well; Hondorp threw in the towel, and, to the surprise of both, she accepted it. The towel consisted of a nod towards a hardware store and his saying, 'What about Golk pounding some fellow's alarm clock to pieces in front of him?'

'Chaplin,' she said. 'Maybe even pre-Chaplin,' and she smiled.

After a pause, he asked, 'Well, what i͜s he working for? What is it that could change our status so?' He'd said this even tenderly.

'We'll see,' she said, with almost corresponding tenderness. 'Sooner than we like.'

Hondorp decided this was enough; he trailed her back to the Parisak Building in silence. Fitch was screening one of the next week's golks. They flopped on the floor and watched it mutely. The victim was a buyer for a department store who was approached by a sinister, though undisguised Golk who talked him into a corner and there flashed a parcel of hot diamonds at him. In five minutes, Golk had flicked off the buyer's thin skin of respectability, enticed him into a deal, and then, after the announcement that they were 'On Camera', marvellously helped him retrieve his front and emerge as a shrewd, but essentially honest type, one who would not only sign the release slip, but who would write to friends and relatives he hadn't seen in years to be on the lookout for the programme. Hondorp found himself feeling the humiliating anguish that the buyer was not feeling, and this suddenly turned into a wide glut of pity for the victims of Golk's trade. He looked across to send this feeling to Hendricks. She was asleep, her head against the back of a prop cart, her face looking not girlish, but fragile, imperilled. The qualms he had been feeling flowed into the ones she had been talking about to him, and he felt in their conjunct force the first tremor in the Golk scaffolding. 'A growth pain,' he said to himself, but the rock he had built on was not where it had been that morning.

II

The next perceptible shift of the rock came two weeks later. He walked in the door one morning to hear Golk's voice call to him over the office loudspeaker, 'Just in time for a screening, my boy.'

'Why's he been waiting for me?' wondered Hondorp. The golks filed in. Golk followed, took his throne, the room's upholstered chair, switched the lights off and the projector on, and Hondorp discovered why his presence was necessary.

The screen filled with Golk in a Harpo Marx wig with a wad of cotton sticking from his right ear. Over him bent Poppa Hondorp, his lipoma swollen and inflamed, his face brindled by the intermittent pressure of his circulatory system. Hondorp felt his insides detach themselves from moorings and churn around until he had to grab a fold of his stomach to down the nausea. Poppa Hondorp was removing the cotton from Golk's ear and peering inside with speculum and reflector. 'There seems,' he said after brief inspection, 'to be no affliction of the auricle, neither tumour—benign or malignant—eczema, serous or sebaceous cyst. From your contortions, I come close to thinking that the source of the Nile, so to speak, is the external auditory canal, suffering maybe under impacted cerumen—wax, for the laity—or perhaps circumscribed or furuncular inflammation, or, and this would be somewhat less likely, otomycosis. I think not, however. My sentiments now incline me to think we may have ourselves a little suppuration of the middle ear.'

Golk's face widened with terror. 'Middle ear, Doctor?' and he caressed his two large ones, his face seamed with cretinous bewilderment.

Poppa Hondorp roared with pleasure. 'Delightful, my friend. A delightful sally.'

'Sally?' asked Golk, but Poppa Hondorp declined the gambit to ask if the ache were chronic.

'Chronic?'

'Recurrent. Repeated. No isolated phenomenon. Has it happened before, this ache?'

'Not this one.'

'Come now. An ache of this sort?'

'Not to me.'

'I see.'

'My dear father suffered frequently from terrible earaches.'

Poppa Hondorp's face crumbled at this. 'Your poor father,' he said sadly, lost for a moment till his professional opportunities were remembered. 'Has he been cured of them, or did——'

'Yes, the Great Reaper took him off,' said Golk. 'Eight years ago, the eleventh of May.'

Poppa Hondorp stared pensively at the blond mop which covered such filial remembrance.

'Many's the long night I spent, a warm cloth pressed against his throbbing ear.'

'Loving,' mused Poppa Hondorp. 'Very loving.'

'You have children, Doctor?'

'A son,' said Poppa Hondorp. 'One son. Name of Herbert.' His tone was elegiac.

'Father and son,' said Golk, as if inscribing a chapter heading on a blank manuscript.

Poppa Hondorp filled in the page. 'A noble relationship.

But packed to the margins, packed, impacted with heart-break. With great heartbreak.' He went to the window, his lipoma pointing angrily askew like an auxiliary, but mutinous head.

'Ingratitude, the serpent's tooth,' urged Golk wistfully.

Poppa Hondorp's lipoma swayed in what seemed negation. 'That's too strong,' he said. 'The matter is not treason, just—how shall I say it?—a carelessness, inattention, lack of thought, but terrible, all terrible. Worse might be better. You would be stiffened to resist. But against so soft a thing, who can push?' Hondorp, on the dark floor, put his head in his palms and rocked back and forth. Around and in his head the sad roar of his father went on, now comparing a father's heart to an hour-glass in which filial love ran out 'the thin neck of old age'.

Hondorp looked up at Golk's actual, bare skull gleaming in the projection machine's light, eyes fixed on the screen with a kind of absorbed detachment, the eyes of an alert, ferocious hound. Hondorp pressed his hands against his stomach and kept his eyes on the screen.

The golk concluded on a large, paternal sigh. There was no reversal, no announcement that cameras and microphones were fixed to opposite windows, that they were On Camera. It was a treatment reserved for only the most successful golks. The lights were switched on and Golk swivelled towards Hondorp. 'You have a gifted father,' he said. 'One in a million.'

'Thank you,' said Hondorp coldly.

'I always give my golks who make the grade a surprise like this. Like a graduation present.' He paused, the weight of the anticipated 'Thank you' hanging over Hondorp. After two seconds rich with silence, he went on: 'Seeing the near-and-dear up on the screen gives you an audience reaction you don't get even from seeing yourself.'

'I see.'

'Well, what do you think?'

'Of—?'

'The golk.'

Hondorp considered. 'There was a disconcerting smear on the top right of half the early frames.'

Klebba reached over Elaine's legs and clapped Hondorp on the back. 'A master's retort, Hondorp. Oh, is he cool, this boy.' Golk nodded approvingly. 'When Golkie showed me Mother Klebba filching change from my desk drawer to pay the milk bill, I nearly cut the throat. Mine. Half of Amsterdam Avenue put the finger on her for a year.'

You mean these little family scenes are shown to—to the public?' asked Hondorp, anger and amazement breaking down his controls.

A roar from all the golks but Hendricks greeted this inquiry. 'Our boy's been bit,' said Benson triumphantly, and the roar took off anew.

'That's the way the mop flops,' said Klebba. 'When you work for Golk, you give *all*, right, Golkie?' Golk nodded with kindly dignity.

'Poppa signed a release?'

'Ask him,' advised Golk. 'You just go home and ask him tonight.'

Hondorp shook his head and indicated that that was exactly what he was going to do.

III

Poppa Hondorp was eating dinner in front of 'This Is Your Life' when his son came home.

'Poppa?'

'Wait till the commercial, darling,' whispered the old

man. Hondorp sat and watched Ralph Edwards interrogating an old movie actress about her second husband's suicide.

'Ups and downs,' said Poppa Hondorp at the commercial. 'Two-column box on the front page when that one passes,' this with a gesture towards a close-up of the actress. 'Imagine it. Maybe a picture—inside-page picture. That's this world. The whole life is lived on the outside. Films.'

'Poppa.'

'Shh.' Ralph Edwards was leading in the actress's elder sister whom she had not seen in thirty-five years. They fell into each other's arms sobbing, and Poppa Hondorp wiped his eyes.

At the next commercial, Hondorp grabbed the bit. 'What did Golk do to you, Poppa?'

'Ahh, sonny dear. I've meant to tell you. Haven't had a chance. Amazing thing happened. In the office comes to me this personage, looks immediately like some moron or imbecile. And who is it? Yes, you know. It's that employer of yours, Golk, with a wig, cameras he gets Nurse Hurwitz to let him put over the windows, microphones coming out of my instruments. This was some amazing thing, I'll tell you. A shock, incredible. Sonny, I cannot thank you enough for it.'

'What?'

'He told me how you'd suggested it, and I told him, "Typical of my boy. He don't forget his father either".'

'You liked it, Poppa?'

'When will it be on the machine?'

'You want it shown, Poppa?'

'Want it shown?' repeated Poppa Hondorp, seeing a discrepancy between his own view and his son's. 'Want it? Of course I want it. A private citizen, suddenly, by the caprice of the gods, enjoying a vast forum like a man of public repute. Of course, my darling. What did you suggest me for if you did not want it shown? This is nothing to paste in an album.'

'My God,' said Hondorp to himself. 'He thanks me.' That his father should relish the opportunity of being the butt of millions believing all the while he was the star guest of some forum programme, this was even worse than if his father had been blackmailed into letting the ridiculous display be telecast. It was incomprehensible to him. He regarded the twin fixities of his father and the machine, the clomping jaws and sucking jowls of the one and the mechanical frenzy of the other. 'Is it for this?' he asked himself. 'For these that I've changed my life? To stuff those jaws?' and his vision was of reciprocal, simultaneous cannibalism. He got up and went into the kitchen, disinterred twelve inches of salami from the salvaged remnants of string beans, steak butts, rotting cheeses, and plastic containers coloured by the last week's gravies and dribblings which Marie's Gascon economy stacked in the Kelvinator. 'No wonder Gascony's almost empty,' he muttered with fury, and, one by one, he dashed the oozing stinks into the garbage pail outside the back door. Weary, he sliced four inches off the salami, poured a mahogany Danish beer into a genuine *Steinkrug*, and brought what his father called the 'TV Snäckchen' into the living-room.

The balm of the Late Show soon closed over his day.

IV

For the next week his father's breakfast discourse centred about his forthcoming 'debut on the mass media'. ('Is he thinking of launching a career?' his son sometimes wondered.) Where young Hondorp had formerly been interrogated about his work along such lines as 'Who's the real brains, Tex or Jinx?' or 'Why did Arthur really fire Julius?' now Poppa Hondorp posed such questions to him as 'Should one speak in the normal tone of voice for best results?' and 'Do certain combinations of colours upset the camera lenses?' These questions, like the others, went unanswered, but this did not upset the old man or deflect him from asking others. He asked now, as he had pronounced earlier, as a way of better digesting his breakfast.

The pace of questioning was advanced a couple of notches after Hondorp announced that Golk had set a date for the telecast. On the actual day, Golk sent Hondorp home early —the programme had an early evening slot—to note his father's reactions.

When he came into Golk's cave the next morning, the opening thrust was, 'Well?'

'He watched it like he watches every other show.'

'What the hell does that mean?'

'With undivided attention. Perhaps he watched it a little better. When Sullivan, or Groucho or Lucy is on, he's practically in the machine. He watched it very closely.'

'Nothing else? How about when he saw himself?'

'There was a momentary recognition, as if he'd seen me somewhere downtown, but that passed. He might have been watching Sullivan, no, someone wise like General Mac-Arthur.'

'Hm.'

'He sometimes laughed at himself, but without any embarrassment that I could see.'

'That's the idea,' said Golk. 'I knew there'd be something special. He saw himself being foolish and disowned himself. The golk acted as a corrective.' He took a green cigarillo out of a drawer, snapped a wooden match across a crack in the desk surface, and lit up.

'He saw a fool,' said Hondorp, quietly, 'but it wasn't himself. He'd go through the exact same shenanigans tomorrow.'

Golk frowned, leaned his head back on the chair rest, and retired into himself. This was dismissal, and Hondorp went into Hendricks's little cubbyhole across the way.

'What are you doing?' he asked for salutation. The golks pretended to no amenities.

'Description.' This meant writing a short description of a forthcoming programme for a prospective sponsor's agency. (Although You're On Camera was going to be sustained by the network for whatever portion of the thirteen-week network contract it took to find a sponsor, the golks were frequently engaged by the network ad men to help sell the programme.) 'How did the old man like it?'

Hondorp told her what he had told Golk, though the recital was more patently venomous.

'Serves you right,' said Hendricks with the contained anger which Hondorp saw as another mark of high style.

'What the hell does that mean?' he responded in what he hoped was kind.

'You don't have to give in to that kind of shit, and you know it. You just trotted up and ate shit because he threw it on your table. You deserve any embarrassment it caused you.'

'May I ask what happened to your little family golk?' he asked.

Hendricks looked at him the way a queen might look at an unknown man who'd made, out of the blue, an obscene sexual proposal to her. Hondorp felt himself strung out on the look for what seemed minutes, until she let him off with 'Don't you think he knows I'd have cut his throat if he'd fooled around like that with me?'

Of the numerous routines to which he was introduced during his first weeks with the golks, Hondorp became most expert at what Golk called his 'embassies'. Golk almost never wrote memos; he sent messages via ambassadors who, as his images, were given more or less *cartes blanches*. Hondorp was soon regarded as an ideal chief of mission, one whose success was grounded in thorough knowledge of the hierarchies of office, network, and industry, the code of injunctions, the table of peccadilloes, of venial and of mortal sins. Even in his second week on the job, Hondorp was sent to the three or four offices which geared Golk's operation with the network's, and with a regularity which endowed him with executive aura in the general eye, Hondorp had always had a kind of presence; now he had radiance, or, as the occasion warranted, magnitude.

Golk planned the missions roughly, but with sweep. There were usually two ambassadors dispatched, and the effect was a scene, one playing the sponge, the other the adamant, or one the whiner, the other the hysteric. It depended on the mission.

As in other cases, Hondorp's partner was usually Hendricks. Their first joint mission had been a financial one. Golk's quarterly allotment was used up: without telling anyone why, he had hired four people as a research staff. It had something to do with his plans for the network show. The Hendricks-Hondorp mission was to gloss over what they would have been unable to reveal anyway, namely the reasons for hiring such a staff, and to get the network to place such a staff on the Golk budget as a regular item. It was not, according to Golk, a difficult mission. 'They can't *not* fork over, or we'd quit. But you may have to take a few whacks for me.' This constituted the whole of Golk's instructions. Hendricks did not, apparently, find them short shrift, but led Hondorp off with businesslike dispatch.

For a change, she wore a dress, a vertically striped tie-silk which, in the fashion she liked, called attention to her height and displayed its contrived gaucherie with expensive materials. The dress also revealed a good pair of legs. 'These execs letch ten hours a day,' she said, explaining the outfit for Hondorp. She led him down a fifteenth-floor corridor past posh apertures and into an office which opened out like a spatula from its reception area stem. Before a great sweep of window glass was an immense curve of light Swedish wood behind which bloomed a head like a casaba melon, a hairless stretch of pale yellow which, to Hondorp, blinking in the bright room, seemed momentarily featureless. When the melon said, 'Come sit down. I'm Lurcher,' Hondorp made out the tiny ripples which constituted nose, mouth, and ears. He took Lurcher's hand and gave his name. (Lurcher almost never stood up: the immense head was the illegitimate fruit of a brief, if globular stem.)

'I know of you,' said Lurcher. 'Eighty-five a week, but I know you. And glad to know you.'

Hondorp slumped in a butterfly chair not made for slumping. Hendricks was already down, exhibiting the legs.

'Nice, nice,' mused Lurcher.

Hendricks outlined Golk's need. Lurcher moved the small pips of his eyes till they pointed at hers. 'In a few weeks,' he said, 'you're big-time, official network, and if you make the grade with a sponsor, I'll be partially free of your depredations. You'll clear your thievery with the agency man. As for now, tell Golk to fire three of them. We'll pay for one. Since when does your outfit use research people anyway?'

'We're branching out,' said Hendricks, stretching a thigh.

'Nice,' said Lurcher quietly.

'Golk has big ideas.'

'He always has had them,' said Lurcher, back without dropping a beat.

'For these ideas he needs researchers,' said Hendricks, borrowing New York syntax for authority.

'Ideas used to come cheaper to him. It's been one of the great things about Golk. He's never really cost anybody money. Hasn't made much, but hasn't cost much. He's a lesson. We use him as a model budget case.' Lurcher scrounged his face till the dark pips seemed to pop out of his head. 'Now he wants to go busting out. I no see.'

'It's not a very difficult thing to see, Lurcher. And the point here is he's never cost you anything, and he's done a lot of good for you, so let him have some leeway without making a fuss about it.'

Hondorp cleared his throat and spoke his first word. 'Surely you people don't want to worry Golk about four piddling researchers just as he's on the verge of making lots of money for you. Or are you just trying to test us?'

The pips seemed to squirt at Hondorp. 'Not a very good line, young man'—Lurcher was two years younger than Hondorp—'but it'll do for today. I'm too weary to wrestle the two of you.' He shivered with pleasure at the sexual undercurrent of this. 'I'll make out authorization. One month, contingent on sponsorship.' The face smoothed out to rind texture. 'I've got an extra ticket for that jazzmatazz at Newport, Jenny. Want to go?' Lurcher had converted to jazz after watching Leonard Bernstein's *Omnibus* lecture on it. He had since bought a thousand albums, three hi-fi sets and hired small combos for solo evenings at home with his girl friends.

'I'll drop you a memo,' said Hendricks. 'Thank you.' The mission was over. She got up, smiled coldly at Lurcher, and led Hondorp out of the office before he could make a more elaborate farewell than 'So long,' called with his back to Lurcher. 'Keep them at arm's length and you'll get what you want around here,' she told him as they moved towards the elevator.

They reported back to Golk who acknowledged the result with a brief smile of gratitude and pronounced Hondorp a subtle negotiator. 'A man of parts, Herbert. You've come a long way in a short while.' The use of his first name dazzled Hondorp, and he smiled the coy smile of infancy. 'Yes sir, you're getting to be a big man.'

'I'm not holding press conferences yet,' said Hondorp as he forced the rapture to seep from him.

'No,' said Golk dourly. 'I don't see the newsies around me either. We don't make the papers any more. At least when we're functioning right. We're what the magazine people call the "back of the book".'

'Sucking hind tit,' said Hendricks.

'Not that it matters,' said Golk with an unhappiness that meant it did. 'Like the Yaddo River, that front-page world's too thin to plough, too mucky to navigate.' He smiled, the phrase restoring his vigour and sense of place. 'Did you ever see that Disney show on atoms?' Catechism was his way of changing course. 'The one with the ping-pong balls knocking into other ping-pong balls until a whole field is full of bouncing balls. Simulated a chain reaction or something.'

'I didn't see it,' said Hondorp.

'It was god-awful,' said Hendricks, who hadn't seen it either.

'I'm just using it as an illustration of the complexity of our position. Every mission, every golk, every move we make influences fifteen or twenty other moves, other positions.'

'The longest way round is the longest way home,' said Hendricks, wishing all of a sudden that she were at the beach at Watch Hill letting the sun knock out the least threat of golkism. For half a second she leaned as if to go only to feel Golk's voice tugging her back.

'Now here's my point,' said Golk leaning forward towards Hondorp and Hendricks perched on opposite corners of his desk and looking in his view like suburban versions of the Medici tomb statues. He paused to contemplate the resemblance before picking up. 'Every request we make of these boys is a threat to their image of perfection —which is routine. Routine means control for them; the new they cannot contemplate with ease. Our old format is a habit for them, and so they feel they're on top of it. They *are* on top of it. They know what to expect, and they can wait us out. For out we'll go, like everyone else in this business, if we stay the same. And they want us out, even though it might look like a break in their routine. It isn't. They'll just come up with another programme, a lukewarm version of our half-hour that'll be a comfortable habit for a while till it drops out. Alternation of the lukewarm: that's their formula for novelty, their proclamation of service to the industry and the nation. Every move we make to fashion a change for ourselves annoys them. Maybe not in so many words——'

'There are indeed a lot of words,' said Hendricks, but Golk only shook his head, flicking off a bug.

'They may even think of it in the term they use for refusal and rejection, "money", but it's the other, and they're going to be gunning for us, watching for us now. They have us twisted around their thirteen-week clauses like strings around tops, and if we don't spin the way they pull, we won't spin at all. So we must pay heed, much heed. We'll start slow, start in old-style, or just slightly different golks, and then, when they've been lulled, we'll hit before they know they've been hit. And then maybe it'll be too late for them to do anything about it.'

'And what is it that they're going to be hit with?' asked Hendricks. Her legs were on the desk now and she coiled towards Golk as if he were charming her with some magic flute.

'Aah,' intoned Golk for response. 'You'll know soon enough. Right now, wait. Sit tight. Say nothing to nobody. Lurcher'll call you in a couple of days: they digest novelty at the rate of a sick elephant, but they'll know something's cooking. So he'll call you. Forewarned is forearmed. A stitch in time saves nine.' Golk rattled off five or six like saws in a distracted, distant manner, a machine that went on sputtering though fuelless. And then, he leaned back against the chair rest and closed his eyes.

They looked at each other and walked out. 'A real bugger,' said Hendricks, but the vehemence mingled with the puzzlement that Golk seldom failed to deposit with her. She and Hondorp looked at each other, a pair of sailors who, their ship gone down, come upon each other swimming in the sea.

CHAPTER FOUR

I

'THERE'S four ways of being successful,' Golk liked to say, 'and they go by way of the suits, hearts, spades, diamonds, clubs.' If he was exercising the autobiographical mode, he would add, 'I've known them all: I've loved up, worked up, bought up, and smashed up. Not that I'm starting to devote myself to looking back. Things are just beginning to break around here. I'm speaking comparatively,' and he would jab a finger towards Fitch or Hondorp or some other measure of comparison.

It was a somewhat oversimplified summary of an involved career, but the direction, at least, was right. It was up nearly all the way. For Golk, no other direction was then conceivable; everything that could have been called reversal or failure was converted into anecdotal roughage.

Of the four suits, Golk particularly overstaked his claim on diamonds: he sprang from neither money, mansion, nor a name. As a matter of record, he didn't even spring from a Golk. The name for most of his life had been Pomeroy. A year after he came to New York, an analyst at a cocktail party told him to change it, and to change everything else as well, girl friends, address, style, told him not to write home to his parents, or, if possible, to forget them entirely. It was a party suggestion, one carried over from an outmoded and disastrous therapy, but Golk swallowed it, whole, and with bliss. For the night hours of a week he debated names from Vanderbilt and Caesar to Smith and Shigemitsu. It was a cut of his new vision that opened Golk to him, a syllable whose vague and ugly suggestibility signalled the way to that montage of the common and unique which bounded the role he began to see himself playing in the world into which he'd plunged, the new world of New York television after the end of the Second World War.

This world was far away from Providence, his origin, and the Boston Store where like, and sometimes alongside, his father he'd clerked, and unlike him, saved and saved to make a break, although not too far from the first breaking-point, the army, where he'd been a non-commissioned star of the Troop Information and Education lectures, a first-class Friday afternoon speaker on 'Argentine: Land of the Pampas', 'Our Policy in the Middle East', and any other world-beating topic the directives pointed to and outlined. And here he was spotted—out in the Oklahoma flats—by a balloon of Pfc., the son of radio network aristocracy, a wise *misérable* who came up after a session of 'The B-57, Architect of Triumph', and said, 'Come see me when you get out,' Lurcher, whose corpulence had in another year foundered in the obesity which secured his discharge, who went back to New York in that spring of 1945 to get a hold in the network world, and who concealed in his oceanic bulk a nerve of recollection which tingled when the big-headed Pomeroy walked into his office two years later, cavernous with anticipation.

The first couple of years were Golk's *Wanderjahre*. His official time was spent with an audience research outfit holed up obscurely in the old network building. (Such outfits didn't become great powers till the fifties.) Not a job which consumed much but complacency, and so Golk moved around the new menagerie of television, handled the new animals, the cranes and crabs, belops and telops, arcs and amps, moved around with the new breed of technicians, actors, incipient directors, producers, agency men, package-dealers, talent-prowlers, and hangers-on, the breed which was beginning to shove the old radio crowd—those too slow or dumb to join them—off the face of the earth.

Half the hours of the day he watched shows, varieties, cookeries, serials, news spiels, quizzes, and he gauged their tempi, camera work, peripeties, assessed their evanescent triumphs and enduring inanities. The assessments he recorded in notebooks, large two-dollar legal notebooks which he filled up at the rate of one a month with observations, ideas, criticisms, hopes; he pasted newspaper clippings in them, wrote up anecdotes, plots, quotations from books, movies, street talk.

It was from this quarry that he drew out the entry which he rewrote one day for Lurcher three years after his arrival in New York. They were more or less celebrating at an anniversary dinner, 'less' because they ate together about once a month without the need of an occasion, and 'more' because this time they were conscious of the fact that Golk had been in New York for three years. The consciousness prepared them for what came from the dinner.

At dessert, Golk took a piece of paper out of his jacket and read it slowly:

Movies, Plays and TV: as far as movies and tv go, you have same possibility of fluidity of place and time, especially filmed TV of course. BUT, in tv, you don't have a large illuminated screen focusing attention of a large audience, nor can you avoid the dispersing of attention a home situation invites—noises, trips to icebox and john—not counting commercials, difficulty of watching smallish picture projected on convex surface. Because of these difficulties, TV demands a smaller canvas, fewer characters, scenes, time shifts than the movies and more or less limited actions. Still, TV has the best of the movie traits, the camera directing the audience to any aspect of a scene, any detail, unusual or otherwise which will best express the flow of the story, plus accentuating music, special visual effects, and so on. So you can hit harder, quicker, and with fewer words than you can on the stage. On the Stage, you need high-pressured action or words to take the audience initially —though the shock of being inside that fourth wall is something—but, since the physical focus is less intense, you can take things at an easier pace. You try for longer, more complicated actions, follow more characters, deal with more themes. So TV and Stage, the thing they share is immediacy. Live TV even has it over the stage, because in news events, or what I'm proposing, there's no script. You're really on the high-wire. However, no spontaneous performance can be too good for too long, especially under the close, movie-type focus. So even the real-laxed, Murrow-Garroway pitch, can't last too long. Entertainment needs more dependable material; the TView can't be organized spontaneously unless life is —and IT isn't. Period. So, the question: HOW best use immediacy on TV? ANSWER: By concentrating on small situations rigged as dramatically as possible, allowing for maximum spontaneity yet putting people, amateur human beings, under pressures which will bring out more or less foreseen responses, responses which will reveal those people dramatically, the artificial calling on the real to produce drama. More than a snooping eye and ear (Eye Ear You—title?), a controlling idea!

Golk looked at Lurcher, his face heavy with inquiry. 'What do you think?'

Lurcher had the same gob of carameled éclair in his mouth that he'd had when Golk started reading. It was the most telling response he could have made. He now got the mess down his throat, spooned up another for fuel, swallowed it, then looked at Golk's questioning head tilted on his in close-up. 'Eye eared you,' he said, and quivered with pleasure, the table squeaking with the movement. 'The title's out.'

'Just a joke,' said Golk.

'Joke or not, out. The idea's—interesting. Not without a certain lack of disinterest.' A quiver. 'If I get it. And I think I get it, though you should learn to mix your theoretical crap with some examples if you want to move anywhere in the upper echelons. You can't explain anything upstairs without an example.'

Golk supplied one. 'Like if there was a cigar in that éclair of yours.'

Lurcher rippled at the threat. 'Good,' he said. 'Dangerous but good. I'm going to take it upstairs. And we'll see.'

'I couldn't ask for more,' said Golk, and his face sloughed off its enquiry, and became again a receptacle for belaboured nourishment.

Upstairs meant, one way or another, Dr Parisak. Ruler of an empire larger than Tamerlane's, more complex, richer, more powerful in its governance of the million or so lives which depended directly, and the billion or so which depended indirectly on it, Parisak was one of the last of those twentieth-century industrial mammoths whose pretence is that no detail is too petty, no development too minor to earn their contempt or dismissal. All network programmes either began as his ideas or existed with his approval, and New York programmes which were being groomed for the network, all, that is, but those of purely local interest, likewise suffered his perilous scrutiny.

Golk wrote a Parisak-type memorandum ('To', 'From', 'In re', '1', '2', '3', 'Thus') based on his conception, had it polished—or perhaps made palatable—by Lurcher, and then by the sharpie Director of Programmes, Domberman, who sent it all the way up to the top floor. A week later, it came back stamped with the gold-laced initial 'P'.

You're On Camera made its début on New York's WPAR two months later as summer replacement for an evening variety show. Golk rented a two-room studio apartment on Eighty-fifth Street off West End Avenue, borrowed money from the station against his earnings, bought two sixteen-mm. cameras, two tape recorders, and a scanner. The station processed the film, but Golk edited it. Indeed, for his first programme he did everything, scouted, planned, set up the lights and recorders, placed the cameras, acted, transported, edited. The mechanics in the garage where the first golk was shot helped him carry the equipment into his fourteen-year-old Hudson. One of the mechanics, Golk's first victim, was Fitch.

A bone-thin, palpitant grease-monkey, Fitch was given a double-talk treatment about the defects of Golk's Hudson. Fitch underwent the scene with a leguminous deadpan which, at the very end, broke for a slow smile of comprehension that something was not as it should be, a smile that established the classic reversal which Golk and the small group of viewers who became his loyal followers that first summer were always to treasure. Two days later, Fitch became Golk's first assistant, his cameraman, set-arranger, actor, factotum, paraclete. His departure from the greasy iron torsos into whose private parts he had poured out the nine working years of his life became the pattern of his master's recruitment procedures. Golk's instinct for the misplaced life, the sheared gift, the convertibility of his fellows was like a poet's gift for metaphor, although more single-minded: the direction of the conversion was always the same: the world's victims were transformed into his own and then into the exploiters of other victims. Golk's eye for the true displacement power of people was guided by his awareness of their ability to generate sympathy and antipathy. This ability was the lode he sought and from which he took his gold.

Fitch had not been the first lode stripped: Golk's first mine had been himself.

II

Golk's progress was guided almost always by principles, not imposed on, but deduced from experience, and then applied with rigour to what eventually served as a further source of principles. In the four years of You're On Camera, there were four major and numerous subordinate classes of golks, and these were worked out not haphazardly but by the hard-working imagination of Golk himself.

The first class or stage—for Golk thought in terms of progress—was the least carefully formulated of the four. The early golks of most of that first summer just *were*, the product of Golk's original, general notion. The second stage of golks was triggered by an experience Golk had had about a month after the first programme was telecast in New York. He was taking his nightly walk down Riverside Drive by the Soldiers' and Sailors' Monument, a couple of blocks from his apartment, and thinking about a paragraph in the New York *World-Telegram*'s TV column praising the show. It was the first public confirmation of his accomplishment, and although the paragraph was far from understanding his real aims, Golk felt that the happy response was itself clear enough indication that he had affected people. He sat on the white steps of the Monument looking up the river towards the Washington Bridge where a plump moon struggled out of the steel suspension wires to queen it over the Jersey neons and palisades. Golk had the habit not of yielding to a scene but of soaking it up, and he was engaged in this process, his body tense with the effort to retain the scene's detail, the river smell and the breeze, the disposition of the moon and the lights and boats, when a dapper little head blotted out his view, asked for a match, and, successful in this petition, went on to a more demanding one. The interruption itself, more than any invidious characterization of the solicitation led Golk to grab the little man's lapels and whisper to him, mob-style, to move out of the way before he got blasted into the Hudson. Into the fair little head flowed a look of such pure terror that Golk brought it up to his own to study it. His study caused the expression to alter first to amazement, then to curiosity and finally to the dispersed truculence which was the face's habitual set. Golk put the man out of his reach as if the night were a garbage-disposal unit, and, with the flash which he had already come to recognize as the sort which really counted for him, he saw that the arousal of such pure looks was what he wanted for his golks.

This was the origin of that second stage of what came to be called golkism. Such golks started appearing during the programme's first regular season in 1951-2, and they centred about such situations as people opening letters informing them that they'd been fired, children at the beach seeing their pails and shovels in the grip of sea monsters, women noticing suicidal types balanced on their living-room ledges. The obituary of the second stage was recorded in a notebook entry in the spring of 1952:

The names of emotions—love, hate, pity, etc.—are just hideaways for the thousand feelings which creep under those labels, or rather, which language tries to bundle away in them. Even the simplest feelings—emotions— wonder what the difference is?—are impure compared with the purity of words.

95

The third stage of golkism had already begun in Golk's second thirty-nine-week season. This stage revolved around scenes which somersaulted victims 'inside out and back again, from laughs to weeps to laughs', as the journal entry had it, through a whole cycle of discoveries. The golks took longer to make—sometimes days—and editing became the crucial part of their production, for only the emotional crests of the cycles were chosen and these had to be ingeniously juxtaposed for dramatic power. The golks centred about such situations as people dispatched on endless errands, errands which were not completed until the victim realized that his own reactions were the object of the errand, that, as he played shuttlecock between two or more golkmen, he was registering the varying forces which they applied to him. The golks involved the use of four or sometimes five cameras, but Golk had local sponsors now and he was seldom bothered by or about expenses.

This third stage brought its own personnel with it: Klebba, a New York hackdriver, who'd been the victim of a golk which saw him trying to collect a fare from a corpse bleeding in the back seat. Once again, the discovery was not chance: Golk's were almost always followed by his discovery of means to slake them.

The third stage lasted less than a year and yielded to what Golk called 'The Quickies', brief, often silent scenes of people coming out of the subway into bright sunshine, eating alone in restaurants, taking walks in the Park, looking at children or in shop windows. The kernel of the scenes was a single close-up, the fingering of a tie or wallet, trembling hands, a smile, the more or less routine response to familiar situations which had been scouted for days by one of the golks. There were shots of passers-by typing messages on the typewriter outside Olivetti, a priest alone at a six-o'clock mass, a waiter picking up an inadequate tip. The programme itself was composed of a group of Quickies based on varied responses to similar situations woven together with narrative commentary by Golk.

The fourth, or penultimate, stage of golkism was concerned with what Golk called 'beat'. The notebook entry which dealt with it went as follows:

Every decent show, every worth-while thing anywhere for that matter, has its own recognizable beat. Music, people's talk, poems, love, meals, the stars. Look at the few real programmes the medium's developed, say Dragnet or a few of the westerns. They've got it. They have (1) regular ways of breaking off scenes—Dragnet has the repeated question and sharp comeback—(2) penetration in depth—Dragnet has the close-up monologue of crook, victim, and witness—(3) development—D. has either the early capture of the wrong man, a long detailed chase, or, the more or less lucky find—'I just saw . . .'—and (4) conclusion—D. has the capture and sentencing. You could write it out like music. If you're in another room, and can't hear the words, just the sound of the programme, you can guess what's going on from the tone and tempo, the BEAT—the slow, broken-up comic interludes with Frank, the hot telephone tips. To discover the rhythm, the BEAT of real-life situations, and yet to put one's own beat on top of them, that's what we've got to do now. Kind of a round, beat over beat, though of course the life beat won't be, or at least isn't, too well defined (unless we had a saint or somebody like that as victim).

The Stage Four golks began in the middle of the programme's third regular season in New York. They were assembled into patterns composed of reversals, discoveries, double-takes, and these were timed, combined with narrative and musical themes, and blended with special camera effects. The results fell into a small number of recognizable categories, so that after a while, Golk could announce at the beginning of a show that the next golk would be a 'fast and looser' or a 'slow shifter' and thus anticipate the rhythmic pattern against which the golk could play minor variations.

It was towards the beginning of the Stage Four golks that Hendricks joined the crew. Her golk was a botched Stage Four which was kept because of her looks and manner, though to Hondorp's surprise—when he later saw the kinescope—the manner was unlike the one he thought of as being her style; she was more the elegant *ratée*, a masterful portrait of a staved-off collapse with the camera focusing on her chewed fingernails and skin, and then islanding her amidst the boxes of shoes in Delman's.

Despite the theoretical failure of her golk—there had been no way to impose a dramatic pattern and still preserve the integrity of the portrayal—the scene was one of the twenty-five or so golks which Golk thought of as his showpieces. That most of these showpieces were theoretical botches amused more than dismayed him. Indeed, in his more and more frequent discussions of golkism, he kept insisting on the inevitability of the gap between theory and results: for him, it was a mark of the importance of his accomplishments.

And the accomplishments seemed more and more important to him. Even before he'd come to the last stage of golkism, he was thinking of his work as a matter of public concern, and he discussed it with the respectful distance usually reserved for older and more conspicuous monuments of culture and civilization.

III

On a Friday morning early in June, two weeks before they were to go on network, Golk unfolded to Hondorp and Hendricks the plan of Stage Five, the stage which was to see the sensational bloom and conclusion of his career. The atmosphere of unfolding was special: Golk wore his navy-blue suit, vintage 1937, worn for every occasion he deemed too formal for slacks and polo coat. Hondorp, summoned with Hendricks into the cave, wondered if they were going to a funeral and questioned the propriety of his own gleaming Chipp's sports coat.

'Let's go,' said Golk secretively, and he led them out across the avenue to the UN Secretariat Building Restaurant high up over the East River.

'Lofty thoughts, lofty places,' he said on the terrace, and he directed a wide glance at the low-lying surroundings, giving the stubby breadth of the Parisak Building an especially contemptuous look. 'We'll have golks,' he said to the waiter.

'Excuse me, sir.'

'Irish on ice with bitters and an orange rind.'

'That can be arranged,' said the waiter.

'Invented it for the occasion,' explained Golk to Hendricks and Hondorp.

Hondorp nodded coldly. He sat as a pupil, a brilliant pupil who holds scepticism in reserve for every word, pruning shears for rhetoric, the hard eye for self-approbatory gush.

Golk stretched his huge jaws and released the initial question of the catechism, his favourite expository method which, in Hendricks's view, he derived from Stalin's sessions with the Comintern. ('It's to shake you up,

99

not to ask you anything.') 'Did you ever read this book by Wilson?'

'!'

'You know the one I mean, this one about the Finnish station.'

'Ah,' said Hondorp. 'Edmund Wilson.'

'That's the ticket.'

'I've read everything,' said Hondorp, in a manner as new and sparkling as his coat. Hendricks observed loudly that his flesh was certainly sad enough, and Hondorp smiled wearily in acknowledgement of the allusion.

Golk did not so much bypass this Abbot-Costelloism as not perceive it. 'I'm thinking about a passage there,' he said. 'Sets Marx and Engels up against Rennin and Mishlitt.'

'Against whom?' said Hondorp.

'Renan and Michelet,' said Hendricks, with slow, pure French tones. Hondorp twisted his lip for independence.

Golk ploughed ahead. 'Here's the point. Mishlitt and Rennin were ambitious in literature and philosophy; they wanted to do good artistic jobs of writing history. Marx and Engels? No. They didn't give a shlitt how the writing came out.' A pause for laughs, and a quick pick-up after none came. 'They wanted to push their stuff, make it count, make it reform, make it explode in the world of here and now, not in the millennium. Remember that part?' Hondorp nodded despite himself. 'And you know what happened.'

'What?' from Hendricks.

'They changed the whole world, that's what. The whole world they changed. You think we'd be having to sit in this UN building here if they hadn't lived? No, we would not. Did they have anything Rennin and Mishlitt didn't?' Pause. 'No. I mean yes. One thing. Direction. They were artists. Wilson says so. That may be the way they're going to survive. BUT, in their time, and for the hundred years which followed, what counted was the direction their force took. They were vectors, direction plus force, and that changed the whole world.'

'That's real news,' said Hendricks.

'Quiet,' said Hondorp intensely. 'What's the application?'

'The application,' said Golk, with the shift to dignified warmth which always took Hondorp by surprise, 'is this. Us. We. We're the application.'

'Explain.'

'We're going to vault the barrier, spring the cage. We're going to instruct, reform. We're going to be the education of the audience. Not the blackboard-and-seats kind, but demonstrators, dramatizers, the portrayers of corruption, connivance, of the tone and temper of the world they live in and don't understand.'

Golk looked Hondorp deep in the eye, digging for approval. He got but a ripple of puzzled surprise which he took—as he would have taken almost any reaction—for what he sought. Any reaction but the one which Hendricks supplied, which was 'Bullshit'.

'No,' he said patiently, quietly. 'Not that at all. It's not at all that. We've been in cages too long, Jeanine. We're not made to be just gawked at. Golked at is what we want, studied, absorbed, remembered, acted upon. Is that right?' No response. 'We're going to tap life out of rocks. They'll sit up and react, and react in a way that's different from the way they react to a play, or from the Kefauver hearings or from anything else, live or filmed, framed or off-the-cuff, Chicago style or the hillbillies. We're getting out of the cages and going into the jungle. That's where we live.'

Hondorp shifted into the rarest of all his gears, interest. 'I'm going to take you seriously, Sydney.' Hendricks's eyes widened. Few knew and fewer used Golk's first name, and she watched to see Golk flinch, but he was nothing but the sculpture of attention, as absorbed now in Hondorp as he was in his scenes.

Hondorp, committed now to scrupulosity and seriousness, realizing that this was the first moment of his life in which what he had to say might determine what someone else was to do, summoned his powers to make a resistance begun more on instinct than not, more as an expression of independence than as an attempt to help his master to a surer footing, a safer course. His head steamed with concentration as Golk watched him, still as a duck hunter in the marsh hearing the first small squawk, so faint he has not yet untied it from his expectation.

'Television,' said Hondorp, 'has all the marketplace attention it needs. That's almost the condition of its existence. My view is that if you've got some contribution to make to the medium, you don't exploit the passive attention of the audience. Anybody can shock a baby, or a television audience. But it's too easy, and the effect is disproportionate to the effort. If you want to contribute, you don't move in the direction of simplifying, vulgarizing your talents in the hopes that you'll accumulate a bigger audience, and a still more moronic one. No. You refine your talents, and either educate your loyal audience or work for a smaller and more critical one whose needs will drive you on to still greater accomplishments. That's what happened in the London theatre in the last years of the sixteenth century, and look what you got . . .'

'Shakespeare,' said Golk, surfacing with a fish in his teeth.

'Among others,' said Hondorp, holding the high line steady. 'But sometimes you get someone like Tolstoy—'

Golk clapped a fist into his palm and groaned. 'What are you throwing Tolstoy at me for? Let's get back on dry land.'

'These are just clear examples.'

'Some examples. Why don't you toss Jesus Christ at me? This is modern times. We're modern people with modern problems.'

'Listen,' said Hondorp, firm, quiet, the village schoolmaster to his old pupil, now governor of the state. 'Plants have roots and soil. Don't throw out examples. Tolstoy had a talent, a big talent——'

'Go on. Give me an education.'

'A big talent that decided it wasn't big enough, or at least wasn't doing the right things, wasn't making enough impact on people. What happened to him?' Golk started to speak but met Hondorp's raised palm. 'I'll tell you. For the rest of his life he was a character, a distinguished jerk, making everyone around him miserable, wife, children, friends, even his crazy disciples, an example which nobody serious followed or could follow, and which people paid attention to only because the example was the wreck of the great Tolstoy.'

'Application?' requested Golk, his mouth a points-down crescent.

'Here,' said Hondorp, and he jabbed a forefinger towards his master's nose. 'There are two sorts of activity, two sorts of talents which move in two different directions. One faces the future, wants to rile its audience, and does so by depositing dissatisfaction, or other emotions which will only be released by some action the audience takes after it leaves the theatre. These are the power men, and they're committed to the future. "Here's the way things are," they say. "Now go do something about them." Then there are the others, the ones who last, the ones who face things as they are, and either reveal them with a perfection which satisfies even people who may be suffering similar things when they leave the theatre, or who manufacture something which doesn't seem to relate to any actual condition but which is itself so diverting, so pleasure-making that it becomes an object of permanent contemplation, I mean one capable of being permanently enjoyed.' The waiter slipped into this tirade with three glasses filled with the lovely concoction Golk had suggested. 'These men,' Hondorp went on, 'face the present, and maybe the past, but in so direct a fashion that the future is assured to them without the ambitious itch driving them on to dubious assaults on a dubious future. My application? Here: Try and be a big man in the market-place, and you'll end up chewing dirt, a Marx if you like with the boils of contradiction showing all over his work, his life and his face—and then only if you're lucky, because in the market-place you take tremendous chances for precious little hope of success, and that's because there, it's the appearance rather than the actuality of worth that counts. That's why it depends on the make-up man, the tin foil, the crazy lights.'

Golk took this mouthful in with—on the whole—respectful care, and he nodded now gravely. 'I don't agree, Herbert,' he said. 'I think I could even argue historically, though I don't know too much there. I mean I think lots of writers like Swift in earlier times wrote to right certain abuses, and I believe they stand up well, but I'm not going to try arguing that way because the way I feel takes care of the arguing. You see, I want to try this other. I want a taste of it, for its own sake first of all, and secondly because in my nose abuse and bad power and dumbness and harsh force itch and smell, and I think that displaying them in our little golks would be a great blow at them. I'm thinking this is the sort of thing we—the medium and us—may have been intended to do. How much real difference will there be between the sort of thing I'm thinking about doing and what we have been doing?'

'You haven't briefed us on what we'll be doing,' said Hendricks, contriving a yawn. 'You've been abstract, exclusively, or else very coy.'

'Yes,' said Golk. 'I'll tell you,' and he drew out a sheet of his notebook paper, set it down beside his drink and read:

People exist in our forced situations far more than they do outside of them. We rig the situation so that it can exhibit——

'That we've heard,' said Hendricks, but Golk just shook his head and went on.

There'll be almost no essential difference in letting that situation be illustrative. All that we have to do is spell out what we're illustrating. We can do that either by narrative, or in a purer sense, by using well-known people, or clearly defined types as victims, and familiar situations which are of public concern. When you show labour leaders and business types in some sort of get-together—having a convivial dinner, say, when the conviviality has sinister overtones of public concern. We're out to write the chapters in this book of concern. 'This is the way things really work,' we'll be saying. 'Look, listen, and don't take the wooden nickels you see being made under the camera's nose.'

As Golk read, Hendricks uncoiled in her chair, and when he finished, she was shifting her head back and forth glaring like a rattler at him. Golk followed her with eyes bright as an infant making for a nipple. For a minute she just shook, and when she spoke, her voice was somewhere between cough and snarl. 'So it really is something new for you this time. It's not even just overreaching what you've been reaching for all along. You've just lost all sense of the world around you. I love rebels. I'm a professional rebel, but I've got controls. I'm aware of the world. Who would let you get a minute of this on the air? How could you keep out of jail a minute if some of it did sneak through? What do you think you are, *The Dirty Drawers Digest*? Disguised as Political Science 31?'

Golk's irises coursed back into the whites. The rebuke thundered at him from a Sinai he recognized.

'Or is this a way out of what you've been doing, an end with a big bang? Baudelaire in the courts. If that's your ticket, remember one thing: you're not in this alone. A whole bunch of us are hanging on to you, and we've been hanging on for no short period—keeping you on earth. What are you thinking of doing with us?'

For a moment it seemed as if Golk were getting up, but it was only that he was stretching the upper part of his body until it gave the impression of being a tent over the table. 'That's enough, I think,' he said, and to her own surprise, she sat back.

'Why a man should have to corral his own shadow, I don't know, but I'll make allowance for the sex of this one.' Hendricks winced. 'Don't you think I'm capable of thinking of what you think of? And have thought of it? Don't you think I've planned this caper? You've been with me long enough to know I don't go shooting off skyrockets for fun. I'm not in business to gratify my fantasy needs. If my stuff isn't on the TV sets, it doesn't exist for me. The plan is clear as springwater, the network's covered, the scenes worked out. It'll take the big shot two weeks to know he's been strewn over the country in ten million pieces. And as for releases, they're unnecessary—if we can't get them, that is. This is a kind of newsreel. When you film a submarine sinking, you don't have to get its permission to record it.' Golk worked himself up, raising eyebrows, waving fingers, his face brilliant in sympathetic illumination of his text, the professor who gives his students something to look at as he expounds. It was a scene contrived for Hendricks and Hondorp, and even for Golk himself, who managed in this fashion to document his own insights. 'We're going to have to be more subtle than the field snake, start slowly, creep up on them, making nothing too explicit, pretend to be doing news but just putting in the technical highlights which will make it clear the news is too new to be news, too private and too dirty.'

Hendricks's forehead creased as if an improper odour had circled the table. 'So,' she said, 'your lousy researchers were serious after all?'

'They've got four or five pigeons lined up right now. Down in Washington, which is the great reservoir of rancour, even more than New York. All those columnists buzzing around stinging people into stories—worse than New York—and the power factions, the ins-and-outs, they're all waiting to spill the other fellow's guts. And our boys are out collecting.'

'Sweet, sweet,' muttered Hondorp, half-way between disgust and relish.

'It's a uranium lode. I was down there maybe two days and my head was clicking like a Geiger counter at a ten-million-ton strike. We've already got three congressmen, the sister of a cabinet member, and a few of the industrialists, including'—and he hesitated here looking at Hendricks—'one of the big Greeks.'

Hendricks, about to say something, held back.

'How did you dig them up?' asked Hondorp.

'It's not hard,' said Golk. 'A letter of introduction here, a kind word there, and then it works like a magnet with iron filings. You pick up one and the rest come in like they were breaking a track record. There'll never be a scarcity of golks down there. The difficulty will be spacing them with the others. You can't just keep pounding away. That's what these newspaper columnists don't understand. They don't vary the tone; they're always crying wolf. No, the principle must always be on top riding its illustration. We'll have to watch out—that I know. On the alert, morning and night. There's a fever here that gets you. I'm trusting you two to see that it doesn't get me, to keep me from blowing my stack over this stuff. If I've been a little too pushy here, it's because I'm not entirely sure what I'm doing. I need you to help me see it and do it.'

He drew donkey ears in the wet ring his glass left on the table, and then sat back and looked out over the river, his features an old, cracking mural on his bent, bald skull. The appeal wrenched Hondorp's reserve from him, and suddenly he felt a discharge of protective love towards Golk. 'It'll be all right, Sydney,' he said, the name coming out of him naturally, and from deeper inside than he would have suspected was possible.

'Let's go,' said Hendricks after watching Hondorp study the great head now almost lolling on the chair-back, as if it were about to be hoisted into place on the papier-mâché trunk of a comic-opera monument. They got up.

As they left Golk, walking through the restaurant's genteel, polylingual fracas, the smells of Indonesian curry and Balkan goulash springing from silver plates to assert themselves like nations in the high, glistening room, they felt as if they were leaving a country which was in the most real sort of way their own, a union of interests that Golk's lolling dome contained and stood for at the same time, the country, Golk, the flag, Golk, the capital, Golk, but feeling this, they felt at the same time the peculiar folly of such allegiance.

IV

Out in the street, the local pressure of a New York summer relieved the pressure of Golk's revelation and appeal. They started walking up Second Avenue, sweating happily, sweating out Golk. In five blocks sweat and dust were their own oppression. 'Let's get the hell out of all this,' said Hendricks. Hondorp concurred with a nod. 'Let's celebrate, like folks celebrate.' Hondorp concurred again, without understanding. Hendricks took him by the elbow and led him out to a bar across the street. They had three brandy Alexanders apiece, then went on to the Music Hall, sat blankly through three hours of Technicolor and the Rockettes, and moved on to the Villa d'Este for dinner. It cost Hondorp—who paid for it, no obstacle being interposed by Hendricks—forty dollars and a head afloat in boozy vertigo. It was Saturday night, and for the first time since his school days, he felt the week-end as a gratifying institution.

It was a muggy evening, and they dripped under a new scarlet moon. 'My God,' said Hendricks firmly, 'let's scram out of this heat.'

'Where?'

'We'll drive up to Watch Hill. We can make it by midnight.'

Hondorp had never made so venturesome a journey, but he saw it as a natural part of the new order. 'I'll call my father,' he said. 'Or should I go home and get some things?'

'Everything's up there,' said Hendricks. 'Just give him a quickie.'

The idea, dipped in the liquor, came out looking newer than most ideas looked to Hendricks. 'It makes me innocent just to think of the ocean,' she said. 'I'm happy just thinking about it.'

'You mean we don't have to go?' asked Hondorp, but she shoved him towards a drugstore, and he went in to make his call. That he took his father away from Sid Caesar was bad enough, but the message seemed to take him away from speech itself. There was a riotous silence at the other end of the line into which Hondorp said three or four times, 'Poppa, are you O.K.?'

Some garbled grunts issued over the line, and then a spate of German of which Hondorp made nothing.

The boozy vertigo helped blunt his father's anger. Indeed Hondorp was tempted to say, 'Dry up, jerk,' but instead, at the first pause in the diatribe, he called, 'Good night, Poppa,' and hung up.

Hendricks drove a Bugatti 41, a car which even on such avenues as Park and Fifth drew gratifyingly envious looks. The car was the same one her father had driven through the twenties and which, every two years, he'd had dismantled and shipped off to the factory for check-ups from which the huge marvel emerged refreshed and resplendent. Hendricks drove the car all around New York, parked it in conspicuous places where it seldom failed to be submerged by goggling pedestrians some of whom, not content with goggling, inscribed delicate sentiments upon it with pencils, pens, chalk, and pointed stones. Hendricks had had the more delicate inscriptions gilded with silver paint, and the car was now tattooed with a gleaming mass of obscenities. It had been the subject of a feature article in the Sunday Magazine Section of the *Daily News*.

For Hondorp, the Bugatti was what a sign would have been to the generation of vipers: it affirmed the somersaulting of his old world, and constituted further invitation to the new dispensation. He was so struck by it as it was chauffeured up the front of the Ambassador by the garage man, that he said nothing, looked even as if it were not dissimilar to the cars he usually travelled in. Hendricks broke a rule about begging responses and asked him what he thought of it.

'Quite spectacular,' he said with a shudder, and slid in next to her as a Baptist into a Roman Catholic pew.

'You don't like it?' pursued Hendricks, ashamed of the solicitation even as she made it.

'One doesn't like the spectacular,' said Hondorp distantly, 'but it excites one.' He sat back while Hendricks drove, or rather exploded out of the city on the East Side Highway. They churned across to the Merritt Parkway and were past Westport before Hondorp said anything but 'I have it' for the tolls.

They were at Watch Hill by two o'clock, and drove along the ocean to a great house which stood on a grassy tip offshore. The moon gleamed enough to let Hondorp distinguish the wind-darkened shingles, the nooks and crannies which were its ticket to the New England shore. There were no lights on.

'They're asleep,' said Hendricks, opening the unlatched door.

The 'they' conjured up Hondorp's old suspicion, and he had a momentary spasm of vision, a husband and children hurtling down the stairs at him asking what he was doing there with wife and mommie. 'Who are "they"?' he asked.

'Grandmother and a couple,' said Hendricks. 'They needn't disturb us too much.'

'From what?' wondered Hondorp, and then his eyes yawned moonsize at the apparent answer to the question. There in the foyer, Hendricks was taking off her clothes. Before he even imagined her naked, she was, softly angular, and more beautiful than he would have guessed from what he'd seen of her, fuller, more graceful.

'Undress,' she said. 'We'll swim New York out of us.'

Hondorp obeyed, studiously, abstracted from old compunction. She took his hand and led him down a grass walk to a square of cold sand and into water so cold that he was yards in before paralysis wore off enough to let him yell.

'Lip it up,' snapped Hendricks as the yell tore up the beach and she gave him an elbow which laid him out in the water. His skin turned inside out; he nearly lost his head. It was like being jammed into an iron maiden. He kicked out for dear life, flailed, churned, slapped himself against the waves. It was marvellous, the most ecstatic state he'd ever sustained beyond spasm. Hendricks was in with him, and then she was swimming under him brushing his stomach and legs and genitals; then she climbed on his back, and they rolled together trying to keep above water, and then sank together, rubbing against each other. They came out together and lay together on the sand, rubbing the gritty texture of their skins on each other, and then making love, with fury. Hondorp felt the top of his head sliding off. And the next thing he knew was total ease, the sense of a feathering sleep.

The next thing was an ache in his side, something whacking his ribs and the pressure of sunlight on his eyes. He shook himself, felt sand under him, made out a smooth brown stick with a rubber cap snapping back and forth against his side, and then, looking up, he saw a square, grey, female head, the lower half of which seemed shot away, the upper half marked by a gold pince-nez from which dribbled half a yard of black grosgrain. The diminished lower half was composed almost entirely of tooth fragments out of which he heard outraged questions about his existence and presence on the lawn. It was then that Hondorp realized he was naked, and he put his hands over his testicles and stammered that he'd been swimming and had fallen asleep, please forgive him, he was a guest of Mrs Hendricks. While the old woman took this in, he leapt up, ran into the house and into another female form in maid's apron who screamed 'George', then upstairs where, on the first landing, he saw Hendricks coming downstairs in Bermuda shorts and tailored blue shirt.

'Just get in, Herbie? You must have jazzed up Grandmother's constitutional. Your stuff's upstairs, second door on the left. Come on down for breakfast when you're decent.'

Hondorp, for a tempting second, saw his fist breaking her head open. Then he jumped upstairs, opened the second door, and saw his clothes rolled together into a bundle lying on what struck him now as a painfully unrumpled bed. He disengaged underwear from jacket and socks, dressed and then sat on the bed to contemplate his humiliation and the ocean. Then he went downstairs towards voices which came from a large screened-in breakfast porch.

Hendricks and the Pince-Nez faced each other over Wheatena, kippers, and scrambled eggs. 'Grandmother, this is Mr Hondorp,' said Hendricks, sweet as early morning sun.

The Pince-Nez extended a bediamonded set of fingers which Hondorp let touch his palm. 'How do you do?' the voice on the beach said as if it had never been a voice on the beach. 'I'm so glad you could come up for the day.' The prepositional phrase was isolated from the rest of the sentence and frozen with injunction. 'I so seldom see Jeanine now that she's a woman of affairs.' The last three words suffered similar isolation but were touched with an almost aching contempt new to Hondorp's palette of social tones.

'It's very good of you to have me, Mrs Hend——'

'I'm Mrs Willoughby,' said the Pince-Nez, her tooth fragments reflecting the sun in such a way as to give the illusion of a smile and yet convey the coldness of Antarctica. Hondorp felt in the mixture a condemnation of his unpressed suit, unshaven face, and—although he could hardly bear to think of it—his uncovered testicles. 'Jeanine is, I suppose, so unused to coming here now that she forgot to brief you on the ordinary details of our secluded life.'

'Yes,' said Hondorp, 'there are a number of precautions which she neglected to take.'

'Eat up, dear,' said Hendricks sweetly. 'Maybe we can have a swim or two before we head back.'

'The water's in the fifties, the low fifties,' said Grandmother Willoughby. 'I wouldn't counsel swimming.'

'I've already been in,' said Hondorp gently. 'Last night.'

'Oh,' said Mrs Willoughby.

'It was colder than any water I've ever drunk.'

'I wonder how you could have survived then. One would think it would have knocked you out.'

'Perhaps it did, Grandmother. Mr Hondorp spent much of the night on the beach.'

The outright rupture caused a moment's silence which Mrs Willoughby broke by rising and saying that she was going into Westerly to shop with George and, if they were still there, might see them for lunch.

'She won't be back till she's telephoned to find we've gone,' said Hendricks. The second Mrs Willoughby left the room, but so loudly that there was little question of her having overheard each word.

'Pleasant little family habits you have, Hendricks,' said Hondorp. 'However, I'd advise you not to screw around with me any more.'

'A little joke like that cements friendships, Herbie. I couldn't resist leaving you for Grandmother. She was the one I wanted to—to golk, not you.'

'I believe you,' said Hondorp, after weighing the matter, 'but don't use me as a prop again.'

Their eyes met over forkfuls of scrambled eggs and softened. 'All right,' said Hendricks. 'I never will.' They each hoisted a forkful of egg in a toast to their pact and alliance. When they drove back to New York after a morning swim, they had become as true friends as either of them had ever had.

CHAPTER FIVE

I

THE network début was, as *Variety* headlined it, a 'Sockeroo'. The Trendex was good and soon became tremendous, John Crosby wrote a laudatory column on the programme's comic freshness, which depended not on the eccentricity of a comedian or the absurdity of a situation, but on the common failings of us all, and other critics followed, Gould waxing philosophic about the approach and Shanley commending the technical inventiveness necessitated by the primitive equipment available for recording the scenes. The Luce magazines and *Newsweek* filled their television columns with Golk, and *Look* and the *Sunday Times Magazine Section* commissioned him to do articles. The programme acquired three regular sponsors and the rigorous respect of the agencies. Within two weeks of the début comedians were doing take-offs on the programme, and the word 'golk'— in small letters—began appearing with its varied significations in editorial columns. Inquiring reporters for the *New York Daily News*, the *Chicago Sun-Times*, and the *San Francisco Chronicle* asked the same question in the same week: 'What would you do if you found yourself golked?' The answers ranged from a matronly 'I'd move out of Levittown like a shot' to a witty 'I'd punch that Golk right in the gums'. The network arranged tie-ups with a toothpaste—'So you'll look nice On Camera'—a beer—'Relax. Be natural for your golk'—and, in a spirit of racy fun, with a brassiére—'I won't be ashamed to meet my golk in a Prettiform Bra'—which was cancelled before it got to the account executive's office. Applications to be on the programme poured into the office where they were thrown away each morning, un-answered. This was bad public relations but Golk's word was, 'They understand so chicken little about the pro-gramme, let them fry.'

The first two network shows were mild, traditional golks, businessmen watching their luncheons fractured by nosy waiters, men in subways finding themselves the objects of glamorous advances. The next two shows were tinted with the new style: the first had the vice-presidents of rival firms eating cordially together while speculating about the advantages of each other's jobs, being brought to this topic by Golk disguised as a potential customer; the second, some-what more 'advanced', as Golk had it, showed secretaries during a coffee break at the Senate Office Building pushed by Golk and Klebba into discussions of senatorial character. The latter stirred a bit of restless speculation in TV columns and in one or two of the national commentators, but only the golks themselves saw what was shaping up.

During this preparatory, softening-up period, Golk, despite the external bloom of his affairs, sulked like Rasselas in the Happy Valley. Only when he fleshed his melancholy for the *Times* and *Look* articles did his eyes snap from the droop which, in his face, meant repression, suspension. The articles themselves, pasted snippets from the notebooks steeped in the high melancholy of Golk's ambition, had, withal their wild raggedness, wide repercussions. The solemn thesis that 'people come over best on the sort of show we work up', was just the sort which the literary editors of dailies, weeklies, monthlies, and even quarterlies could blow into a big storm, and did. The articles were closely followed by the showing of the Dammer, Long, and Castelvetro golks, and then You're On Camera became Golk's dream of it, a national sensation.

Mrs James Dammer tried to keep out of her husband's way, but it was difficult. He'd had his bi-weekly hour with the President in the morning, and the self-deprecation such meetings involved exhausted his small stock of patience. Mrs Dammer suffered him at lunch, played cribbage in the solarium with him till two, read *Framley Parsonage* to him till three, and then nearly got away to go to the market when he said that he'd like to go with her.

'I haven't been shopping in years,' he said. 'It might open my eyes a bit to see how much little things cost.'

Mrs Dammer trembled at the prospect. She urged her canary nose higher in the air and shook it a little. 'You'd just hate it, Jimmy. Even our little Georgetown market's unbearable. People just push you along, snatch fruit out of your hands, drop things over your clothes, sneer at you. It's really unbearable.'

'You should send Burton, my dear. I had no idea. I can't imagine why you go.'

'Mortification,' said Mrs Dammer. 'It's a weekly mortification, though at times I can hardly sustain it even for that.'

Dammer pinned his Angelico blue eyes to his wife's. 'To think how much our situations really correspond, Emily,' he said with an irony so slight only she would have caught it. 'Yours in your little way, mine in mine. You're spared nothing I'm spared but the fearful consequences of your decisions. We suffer alike.'

Mrs Dammer touched a soft hand to her husband's sand-grey crewcut, the feature which, with his large, tender eyes and plump cheeks, the cartoonists most sported with. 'You're too generous, dear. I can't see you wasting time with me, time the nation needs so much more than I. If I read of some emergency in the paper tomorrow, even if it weren't something that was your concern, I think I'd just be miserable to think I might have been indirectly responsible for it.'

'I'll get my hat, Emily,' said Dammer springing from his chair with an old track-and-field man's flicking grace. 'We'll ease each other's burdens, and let the country take care of itself this afternoon. There aren't any indispensable cocktail parties today, and only that soirée for the Duke of Messina tonight. I'm a free man,' he called from the door, salting the last with the much thicker irony which, at cabinet meetings, was his trademark. 'Dammer doesn't say much, but there's always a twist to it,' the Vice-President had been quoted as saying in a recent Letter from Washington.

Mrs Dammer sat back in the sofa. 'Oh well,' she sighed, 'He'll be in Formosa Saturday, and then I don't need to go tonight. In fact, I don't remember being asked. Maybe they were working from an old list,' for the Dammers had been married, each for the second time, but two years ago, and not a few times since Dammer had been invited as an eligible widower to fill out—though with spectacular distinction—a table, usually at one of the older Washington houses. But being left out did not disturb Mrs Dammer, for she could barely tolerate her husband at parties, let alone one attended on the night of a session with the President. Dammer was a notoriety at Washington parties, and considering that he drank little and never flirted, this was peculiarly rare. But then Dammer's vice was peculiar, or rather, the extent to which he practised a familiar Washington vice was. The vice consisted of not noticing, apparently not being able to notice, any person who was not distinguished by either fortune, lineage, or position. At crowded parties, it was the sport of newspapermen, minor government officials, Committee counsels, Supreme Court Justice clerks, chargés d'affaires of the smaller Latin-American countries and the like to attempt to engage Dammer in conversation and to observe, and then later report on the machinations which extricated him from the ignominious encounters. He would spill drinks, suffer coughing fits, recognize old friends across the room, make for the bathroom, or simply lift his grey faun's head above his assailant's—he was very tall—and pucker up as if there were a mess of dead fish at his feet.

Mrs Dammer was not the most cordial of women, but she was never deliberately without good manners, and her husband's patent discard of them on such occasions caused her pain and humiliation. 'What will he be like at market?' she wondered as she pulled a bellcord to summon the chauffeur.

But the marketing, to her immense relief, passed fairly easily. Aside from interrogating Frank, the grocer, about the wholesale prices and counselling him about his mark-ups, and from somewhat more elaborate interrogation of the only other customer in the store about her shopping habits ('Do you buy seasonally?' and 'Do you try to have your family eat eggs and fish once a week?' to which the answer was 'I live alone if that's all right with you') the expedition was unmarred by incident.

None the less, after a dinner which was consumed by the salted denunciation of an Assistant Secretary of Labour's wife, and an hour of Pig during which Mrs Dammer suffered a bloody nose when she jammed a finger into a nostril instead of just to her nose, she was not only ready for bed by nine o'clock but almost ready for another session in her rest home.

'Have a pleasant evening, dear,' she said, leaving her husband at the stairwell, 'and do make my apologies.'

'Good night, Emily,' he said. 'If any Almanach de Gotha

degenerate does anything unspeakable, I'll save it for break-fast.' The tone wasn't genuine: both the Dammers came from families which were neither provincial nor distinguished enough to take any attitude towards European nobility but one of respect.

He consulted his calendar, noted 'WT' for 'white tie', dressed, called down for Burton, and was driven to Demicapoulis's Chevy Chase mansion.

The house was almost his chief interest in the soirée. Since he had personally uncovered the arrangement whereby the Greek was reselling to the government what had been its own scrapped property at a four thousand per cent profit and had hastily plugged the gap (or tried, as a matter of fact, for the Greek had as usual managed to come out of the negotiations even more handsomely), the Greek had remade what had been an inconspicuous fifteen-room British Embassy Annex into a forty-room monster, buying up fifteen houses on either side which he razed and converted into thick lawn. His profits from the scrap venture were said to have been almost entirely invested in the project.

The car drove up an alley of cypress (brought in from Florence in gigantic freezers, it was said), through a gate at which he had to be identified by a guard ('This is probably against the Alien Property Act,' muttered Dammer, 'maintaining a foreign troop outside of embassy grounds,' and he decided to have this checked on), to an immense spread of yellow stone which struck Dammer as being extraordinarily ill-lit for a great fête. He was somewhat reassured by a line of chauffeured limousines on an adjacent green and an operatic-looking footman standing under the lighted centre door. A similar form opened the car door, another the front door, and inside he was told by a butler that His Highness was receiving in the Timeo Danaos Room at the left. 'They don't quite catch on to Washington procedure, these lesser royalties,' thought Dammer as he went by himself across a large, dimly lit receiving hall into the room towards which he'd been directed.

'Can I be so early?' he asked himself. There were less than ten people clumped in the centre of a tremendous circular room, brilliantly lit in the middle, infernally black elsewhere. Dammer shivered for a second, and almost turned around to go back when a figure detached itself from the clump and called across the forty feet of polished floor, 'Come join us here, do.'

Dammer's head arched for a moment on his neck, but as there was no one close enough to him to stare over, he made his way to the group. There were four women (one a Negress or Indian) dressed, amazingly enough, in identical yellow evening dresses, and all wearing what seemed to be great sapphires in their ears. There were five or six men including the bulky little man with a great head and John-Calhoun-type sidewhiskers who had called to him. The men were dressed in business suits.

'How do you do?' asked the man with the whiskers. 'I'm Rinaldo.'

'How do you do?' Dammer managed. 'I'm James Dammer. I wonder if I've come to the right place.'

'Demicapoulis's,' said the other. 'Lent to me, the Duke of Messina, for a few months' stay. Very handsome of him.'

'It is the right place then,' said Dammer. 'I'd understood there was to be a large party here.'

'Just some friends,' said the Duke. 'The large party is *next* Tuesday, I think.'

'Ahh,' said Dammer, more relieved than embarrassed. 'Then I've intruded. I've made a mistake, or my secretary has. It's very rare. I trust that you'll forgive me. Perhaps you'll let me come back next week,' and he made as if to go.

'Please do stay, Mr Dammer. Meet my friends and have some *vin de Messine*. We make it ourselves. Let me present you to everyone,` and the Duke unloosed a series of garbled names which with one or two exceptions clinked with the syllables of nobility.

'Delighted,' said Dammer. 'It's really a relief to be one of a small party when one has anticipated a mob. Especially after a day such as I've had.'

'Ah, you've had a difficult day, you poor man,' said a tall blonde in a seductive, gently foreign voice. 'I hope nothing disastrous has happened.'

'Nothing like that,' said Dammer smiling, and noticing that the others were giving him complete attention. 'A conference with the President usually makes me tense.'

'Yes, he's an intelligent fellow,' said a dark, sour-looking man.

'That's true as well,' said Dammer hesitatingly. 'The tension comes more from—as you can all imagine—one's knowledge that as one presents, at last, long-cherished and carefully worked-out plans, it is the point of no return. There can be no more wobbling or hesitation. The President relies on one; you have an hour to make your report, and the next hour may see it turn into—well, you can imagine. And how do you find the United States these days?' he went on more or less to the blonde and without the slightest tonal indication of the topical switch.

'Uninteresting,' was her response, uttered in a some-what different accent, which only deepened Dammer's discomfort.

'And may I ask,' he went on, 'whether the charming dresses you and the other ladies are wearing are some sort of uniform, a caste mark of some sort?'

'We got them wholesale,' said the Negress.

'Ha ha,' was Dammer's response.

'Glad you like them, Senator,' said the blonde.

Dammer curled away from the word that touched the bitterest incident of his life, and said that, unfortunately, he was not and had never been a senator. Dammer had had one fling in politics: his St. Louis law partner had garnered organizational support for him after he and Dammer had won a famous case, and Dammer campaigned for the senatorial nomination. He had been beaten by a folksy war hero in the most one-sided primary victory in Missouri history. Dammer could not see his old rival's name in print without feeling nauseous. The word 'senator'—despite the long, inuring years in Washington—had some of the same incantatory power, which even now, in the presence of foreigners who could be presumed not to know of the humiliating campaign, spilled anxiety into Dammer's eyes. Dammer himself was the only one who realized that the fetishistic sensitivity was at the root of his celebrated party manner.

The fatal instinct of women—this was Dammer's view of it—drove the tall blonde towards agonizing exploration of the infected tissue. 'I'm somewhat relieved at that, sir,' she said, the only trace of accent now being a three-syllable pronunciation of the past participle. 'Would it be unkind of me to say that the quality of the American legislators is at times something to be deplored?' As long as the terrible subject was pursued, thought Dammer, it was at least being pursued in the right direction.

'It might not be too disloyal of me to say that there have been times when I've felt the same way about this matter as you, Countess,' said Dammer, the title coming to his lips although he'd been given no reason to use it.

'Mmm,' was her response, and it was accompanied by a head motion that seemed noble, indeed regal, beginning as it did at her eyebrows and ending not much below them.

'There are indeed what I might call actual roughnecks in the great chamber.'

Dammer followed this curve and nodded, unsure whether he should relax and give vent to his spleen or divert the conversation from what could turn out to be a blast at his own interior. But hesitation decided it for him: the very name of his personal nemesis was in the air. The strange blonde spat it out of her mouth with a distaste that to Dammer seemed an articulate version of that which he had publicly suppressed for a decade. 'And he has such a following here,' she went on, bringing Dammer's heart around her words and stretching it painfully. His head started arching, the instinctive move towards freedom, but there was nowhere to go here. They were islanded, the two of them, in a strangely large and powerfully illuminated island of attention. At his breaking point, Dammer burst out, 'In our country, Countess, a certain brand of viciousness has always enjoyed a remarkable welcome. Vulgarity to the vulgar, baseness to the base. The mob smells the wolf which stinks of rotten meat and they're transfixed by the smell. Yes,' he went on, his great blue eyes rolling slightly in the grey, impeccable face, 'the rotten meat draws the pack.'

Around him, around these words, Dammer remarked a vast envelope of silence, felt the steam of arc lights bearing on his head. 'Have I said too much?' he asked himself looking at the wise looks of the foreigners enclosing him, feeling in a minute that more than their observation was pressing him. Suddenly there was a stir in the black periphery of the room, and Dammer turned to see moving towards him out of the dark what at first seemed to him the incarnations of a nightmare, large, many-eyed monsters which, as he watched, battered with astonishment, turned into large cameras dollied out by men in slacks and sports shirts. Now he saw that the mysterious illumination came from immense stage lights fixed to long curving poles, and that the people who composed the island of attention were now but smiling individuals relaxed out of foreign postures into what were to Dammer clear American types, that the large-domed Duke of Messina was pulling off his sidewhiskers and saying in the most American of voices, 'You're On Camera, Mr Dammer. This is a national television programme.'

The next seconds were the longest in Dammer's life. 'Ha, ha, ha, ha, ha,' he managed to get out then. 'Ha, ha, ha. Marvellous. Wonderfully funny,' he pushed out of the river of sand which was his throat, and he clapped Golk on the shoulder to keep from keeling over.

And then he was gone, though, with remarkable strength, he turned once at the door to call back, 'Good game. Swell fun. Good night all. Good night.'

III

It was a wonder to all who knew anything about George Armbruster Long that he had managed to stay in Washington so long, let alone in positions of some influence, if little authority. Long was not yet fifty, but he had been in official Washington for nearly thirty years. He had arrived directly after flunking out of the University of Virginia in his junior year. He had made up for this difficult achievement by marrying the only daughter of a brain truster and getting attached to his father-in-law's Washington staff. In Washington, as if to compensate for his Charlottesville career, he became something of a student. The new political orders of the twenties and thirties became his passion, and the newer they were, the more passionate he was about them. Of the very newest, German National Socialism, he became one of the first American apostles; in fact, early in 1935 he addressed a letter (on official stationery) directly to Hitler, in which he made application for a post in the German government. 'Any position in which I can be of service will do,' he wrote, although he suggested that his experience in Washington might qualify him for one in the American Affairs Section of the Auslandsabteilung. (Except for this word, the letter was in English; there were limits to George's studies.) Four months later, he received an answer which his father-in-law's German maid translated for him. It was a short note: 'The Führer, Herr Hitler, appreciates your interest in German affairs, but regrets that he must inform you that his staff is complete.'

Two months later, George, on fire with old errors and new passion, wrote to Moscow. The response to this was less remote. A month later, a hand poked itself out of a Ford coupé in front of his apartment building and waved at him. George approached, was told to get in, did, and was driven down to the Union Station car lot. The driver was a man of fifty dressed in an old tweed topcoat buttoned from chin to knees.

At the station, parked in the middle of a row of cars, the man turned to him, transformed, his timidity shed along with ten or fifteen years, his topcoat unbuttoned enough to reveal the glint of a uniform. 'You wrote a letter to Moscow on 19th March last?' he asked.

'Yes I did,' said George. 'I gather it arrived.'

'Correct. The question is, "How serious was the letter?" We've looked into your dossier a bit, and you do not seem to be either a prankster or an agent, but we don't see that you're a Marxist either. Are you a fool?'

'No,' said George sincerely, but saying it, he began feeling a disturbing discrepancy between the nature of the question and his own passion for social justice and unsentimental revolution. The hard, querulous head sticking up out of the ambiguous glint, the rows and rows of cars, these worked in him depression, whereas his emotional goal was elation. 'But I've changed my mind since the letter,' he went on. 'I'm going to be a student of Soviet affairs, not an active participant in them.'

The topcoat was rebuttoned, the face aged, and timidity oozed back into it. The door was opened and George refrained from asking what he wanted to ask, which was, 'Could you drive me to the Carlton?'

During the next few years, George shifted from Congressional Committee to Committee, usually as a researcher or investigator. His next real boost came when his father-in-law split with the President and left Washington to become an executive with a South-western oil company. George went along to Dallas, and stayed to learn the rudiments of the oil code, and much more than the rudiments of what oil men needed from Washington. He returned to the city as a registered lobbyist, and for the next few years performed easy tasks with easy charm. He made money enough to take care of what were never extravagant needs, and then he began to itch again for government life and power. He took a minor post in the Treasury Department and from here worked himself over to the Petroleum Section of the State Department, which is where he was at Pearl Harbour. Then, despite his departmental exemption, he chose the path of valour, and was commissioned a staff officer assigned to Petroleum Affairs with G-2 in Washington. After the war, he moved back across the Mall to the Department. Here he stayed through two Democratic and one Republican administration, although, in the latter, he felt an occasional cutting wind pass close by him. Just before the start of the second term, the wind whistled with perilous precision: he had written a memo on tidelands oil which had close verbal resemblances to the brief of one of the less subtle lobbyists, and only the pressure of the coming campaign diverted serious attention from him and it. But he knew that he was trembling on the razor's edge, and he began coasting around for an area of extra-governmental repose. Now, in late June, he felt that he was on to something.

..A representative of the great shipping magnate, Demicapoulis, had come to him with a suggestion that he might act as liaison man between Demicapoulis and the Texas oil firm with which he had been associated to work out a tanker arrangement. (George was somewhat surprised at the particular offer, since he had been one who had advocated a 'crack-down' policy on Demicapoulis in the affair of the resale of government property to the government; still he thought it unlikely that this fact was widely known.)

On Tuesday he lunched with Demicapoulis's representative, Theopopos, a small, bulky man with a great bald head and a thick red, almost artificial-looking moustache. They met at Theopopos's suite at the Mayflower. George reviewed his whole career under the pressure of the cautious Greek, and then declared what he thought official policy would be towards the arrangements. The interview, held in the marvellously bright suite, went swimmingly.

IV

Andrea 'Dove-Eyes' Castelvetro, muscleman turned negotiator and headed for the top of his profession, was just back from a difficult Washington session with a Senatorial subcommittee when a phone call from the Atropos Shipping Line opened up to him a prospect so lush that the strain of endless reiterations of 'I must respectfully decline to answer on the grounds that it may tend to incriminate me' passed from his handsome face and deposited there instead that seraphic, forward look which had gained him his familiar nickname. For four years he and his concern had been vainly trying to work out an agreement with Atropos, only to be foiled by a large, and spectacularly well-armed local union devoted exclusively and far beyond the usual call of duty to the selfish interests of the management. Now, according to Theopopos, the company's new representative, the cost of that exclusive devotion had reached the point where it was less expensive to make the standard working agreement with Castelvetro's union.

The preliminary meeting was to be held on Theopopos's yacht anchored across from the great Joseph Kennedy yacht in Oyster Bay. (This juxtaposition was taken by Dove-Eyes as a wonderful bit of play in view of his recent interrogation by Kennedy's son. 'I never been easy with Greeks,' he told his driver on the way out to Long Island, 'but they got a great nose for humour.')

Down at the harbour, he put on the commodore's cap he had been instructed to wear, brushed specks of car lint off the fifty-dollar white flannels he'd bought for the outing, and after making the signal, two taps of the cap's visor, got into a motor-boat and was driven out to the yacht, a seventy-foot power boat that—he was piqued to see—was larger, if less elegantly fitted out than his own boss's boat. Theopopos, a strange-looking fellow who looked strangely familiar to him, helped him up on deck and walked him around to the quarterdeck where under the hot sun was a table laid out with caviar, sturgeon, and champagne.

'A good way to have a conference,' said Castelvetro with the amiability which had lifted him so rapidly from the ranks of the musclemen.

'That's the way we operate,' said Theopopos, 'the way we always want to operate.'

'No reason why not,' said Castelvetro, meeting the by-play with his usual agility.

Theopopos nodded sweetly and suggested that they get right down to work. Through their huddled heads, the bare rigging of the Kennedy yacht shifted easily in the sun.

V

The reactions to the three great golks of Stage Five brought smiles even to Golk's face. Every newspaper report, every commentator's spiel, sank a new well of satisfaction deep inside him, and for days he did little more than beam and read and listen to that which made him beam more. When the *Times* reviewed the three golks, showing how the public image of Dammer, the unruffled advisor extraordinary, lay shattered before the presentation of his prissy snobbishness and awkward, malicious innocence, and wondered in the cloister of the editorial page about the thirty-year tolerance of Long's uncamouflaged finagling and Castelvetro's unsheathed corruption, Golk saw the certification of his programme's power. Other issues were raised simultaneously by the newspapers and by public figures: these concerned the propriety, even the legality of You're On Camera's exposure.

'What triumphs,' Golk murmured sweetly, the day after the Castelvetro golk. 'The *Telegram* says some congressman's brewing a bill to outlaw us. He's going to talk to the President about it.'

'What'll this do to us?' asked Hendricks.

Golk looked up from the newspapers and shook his head. 'We'll take it to the courts as the freedom of the artist to present the world in his own terms. It'll be a case for the law-books, something for these dumb buggers to test their teeth on. Listen to this bilge,' and he drew out the editorial page of the *New Orleans Press-Dispatch* and read it out *à la* Gabriel Heatter.

What was a fictional nightmare in the pages of *Nineteen-Eighty-Four* has become reality. A reality that proves, however, to be more garish a nightmare than even George Orwell described. Orwell pictured a world in which men were constantly spied upon by the secret police of a super-state. On the Parisak Network, a New York comedian with the improbable name of Golk displayed not to the secret police but to the entire nation—or, at least, to that large portion of it which is watching his sensationalist programme—the private behaviour of individuals, individuals who are sometimes men of international importance. Their behaviour is under none of the constraints which awareness of being spied upon put upon the behaviour of people in the Orwell state, and thus what the world sees reeks of the jungle. At the conclusion of his programmes, Mr Golk appears before the camera to say, 'Next time, maybe you'll be the star of "You're On Camera".' Our reaction to this is one of rage. So serious an invasion of private life has probably never before been held over the heads of Americans. Golk appears before us as a comedian. It seems to us high time that we took him very seriously indeed.

'Improbable name,' snapped its possessor. 'Hopheaded hypocrites. Half their waking hours are spent rooting out the world's dirt, getting their mangy stories, pumping the news out of everybody's guts, and the rest of the time they complain about people who really turn the insides out.' But the smile spoke for the bliss which he lapped up from the editorial.

'Don't tread air, Golk,' said Hendricks who was writhing

in the display of self-gratulation. 'You know what the Greeks said.'

'Demicapoulis?' said Golk. 'Don't be a dope. He's so nuts about what we're doing he can hardly contain himself. We shipped him another kinescope an hour ago. Your old ex's boss was a gift of God, Jenny, and that old letter of yours opened him up for us. I owe you for that.'

'I'm not talking about that thief,' said Hendricks, wound up even more by Golk's hurtling ignorance. 'I mean the ones who said, "Pride goes before the big fall. Don't crow on the dunghill." I'd watch it, Golk. I smell consequences.'

Golk's great head seemed to let air; the seams showed and he spoke softly, gently. 'Let me rant a little, Jenny. It's the way I relax. We've had a long haul uphill. Of course, there're going to be consequences. What's the point of doing anything if it's not going to have consequences?'

Half under his words, she said, 'I know. You fish to eat.'

'They're not going to let us go on like this for long. I'm aware of that. Who even wants to? We'll move on, but meanwhile we'll have done a noble stint, a clean job. Something nobody'll ever take away from us. I'm proud of these golks. They were hard to assemble, harder to pull off, but we worked them. So let me crow a little. If I've got the surplus energy to do that, it's not going to kill anyone.'

Golk crowed for a few more days. More than crowed. As a maniac fit comes on, pools of energy blasting out in the body, drumming joy in the head until the world looks all bright, all yours, so Golk pranced high surveying studio and city. While crowds looked on and newsreel cameras followed, he led the golks on a tour of the city monuments, and had Fitch take Aunt-Mary-shots of him with them. His great head blotted out the Statue of Liberty's, blew crumbs to pigeons on St Patrick's steps, dangled in mock terror from the Observation Tower of the Empire State Building, kissed Washington's foot on the Sub-Treasury steps, held fish in its teeth while the Central Park seals goggled with desire, rubbed noses with movie blondes in the Colony, imitated a screaming horse before the Museum's Guernica, ducked fly balls during batting practice at the Polo Grounds, and everywhere, talked and talked and talked, about the city, the weather, the sights, the condition of men and business, the purpose of entertainment, the art of television, and the universe of golkdom. In these days he seemed almost never to be still: legs and arms and mouth kept in motion as if future motion depended on never stopping.

Then, he relaxed, and went back to the office to review the Stage Four golks they were using to bridge the explosions. He was just about to head out for a cruise in Oyster Bay (Demicapoulis had put his yacht at Golk's disposal for the summer) when Hondorp jogged into the cave flapping a piece of paper topped by a golden 'P'. 'It's all over,' he said mournfully.

Golk took the paper, and then said before really seeing it, 'I told you they digested novelty like sick elephants. It must have been that forty-five Nielsen that held them back this long.'

'Castelvetro and Long have five-million-dollar suits filed——'

Golk coughed up a huge laugh. 'They don't have a leg to piss on.'

'Lurcher says Parisak is going to settle with them for half a million apiece and is going to make a public apology for the golks. On network. On Golk time. Dammer has the FCC looking at the network charter.'

Golk's head rocked back and forth like a sick bell-clapper.

'The battle of the giants,' he said after a minute. 'Well, we waved that old lion by the tail longer than most.'

'Where do we go from here, Sydney?' asked Hondorp sitting on his corner of the desk.

'I wonder,' said Golk. 'I take it they want to inspect our films before we put them on the air.'

'That's it.'

'Too bad. I wanted to do the Yankee-Kansas City one before we folded. Well, we'll just do some old-style golks, take the rating loss, and wait for the axe. Or we could go ahead and make a few whoppers, and just hold off with them until someone with guts started up a network which'd just tell everyone to go screw themselves.'

'Are you joking?'

'Ruminating.'

Hondorp flapped the paper back and forth. 'The sentence of death.'

'Not so gloomy, Herbert. Even in our time, they can't keep a good man down.' This earned the sort of laugh he usually solicited in vain. 'No. If they renew——'

'If they renew.'

'If they renew, we'll do a series of quiet, well-made affairs, and then, just kind of by accident, when nobody's looking, we'll slip in a bomb or two, and then cart the heads out of the way before anybody can trip over them.'

Hondorp intoned a curtain speech to the effect that when the dead didn't know they were buried, it was time for the living to clear out. But Golk was out of things now, his head lolling back against the chair rest. After a few seconds in which Hondorp paid it the familiar respects of contemplation, he went out for a drink and conference with Hendricks.

Or started out of the building at any rate, for the way was blocked by a raucous embolus of photographers flashing cameras, hurling orders and questions, all in the tone of insult and assault which gave them the collective identity of a species known and reviled over the earth.

'It's our own medicine,' said Hendricks. 'Except that here it's the disease.'

Hondorp paused to give his face to a few million readers before ducking back in the building for the Bacardi in Hendricks's desk.

They sat by a window overlooking the steaming miles of Queens across the river. Rising in the heat, the injured colours of the city seemed from their height to be refusing association with the objects on which they existed; to Hondorp the view was that of an endless canvas by Pollock or de Kooning, and with even less relationship to life. They drank the Bacardi from eighteenth-century Baccarat glasses Hendricks had taken from Watch Hill.

'Well, here's to Golk,' said Hondorp, ticking her glass at the third refill.

'Got what he was looking for,' said Hendricks.

Her gold head outlined against the suffering canvas of the city was the only thing in the universe clear to Hondorp. 'That's supposed to be good,' he said.

'If you know what you're looking for,' she said, watching him watch her, and letting the rum rest and glisten on her lips for his pleasure.

'I know what I want,' he said firmly and touched her knee with his palm.

'That's too easy,' she said, 'and I'm too tired to dance on a coffin.'

'We're exaggerating. He's eternal.'

'Not his coffin. Ours. The coffin of the programme. He's right about keeping the good man down. There aren't enough around to bury him. It's us, his format, that are on the lip of hell.'

'And just as I was beginning to like it all,' said Hondorp, his vertigo dipped now into gloom.

It was true. Hondorp had eaten it up, publicity, flash-bulbs, and all. The total reversal of his obscurity, the grotesque extrapolation of his choice tickled him no end. His father goggling at Page One of the morning Scripture, the interviews, all had assured him, 'You're alive. They care for you. They want you.' He toyed with the sensational world, provided bait for it. At the airport the other day, he had made an arm-in-arm exit with Elaine through a canopy of bulb-flashes, gone into a taxi with her, and while the bulbs popped off the taxi windows, put his tongue into her mouth. 'Let them debate this in Memphis,' he said to her.

He had brought her home to dinner, his game with himself becoming then a game with that minuscule section of the public constituted by his father. As it was every evening now, his approach to the apartment building had been a triumphant entry. The doorman waved aside three auto-graph hounds and then applauded with the elevator operators as he entered. Because of Hondorp, the house was the talk of the street: 'Hondorp, one of Golk's top assistants, lives here.' Elaine was recognized as having been touched with the same magic, and the fact that she had been more than touched with the tar brush, in a house and along an avenue in which the only such specimens wore uniforms, was nothing alongside the fire of such celebrity.

For Poppa Hondorp, the presence of a guest at dinner was the overriding fact. It had not happened for years, and never as far as his son's friends were concerned. (There were none to invite.) The fact that the guest was a '*Schwarz-erin*' was so fantastic an embroidery of the initial fact that it took him to the middle of the salad to register it, and, by then, he had grown accustomed to Elaine as guest, his son's colleague and fellow celebrity, and, as much as his limited capacity enabled him, as a person. For someone who had never entertained a Negro or treated one as a patient, it was a surprising adjustment.

'Have you been down in Florida, Miss Parsons?' he'd put to her between forkfuls of vinegar-soaked lettuce.

'We don't have time to travel, Doctor. Working for Golk is a full-time job and then some.'

'You must be one of the fortunate New Yorkers who have sunbathing terraces,' he pursued.

'Oh, no,' said Elaine. 'This complexion is natural.'

'I see,' he said slowly, eyes widening. 'Well, it's just one of those things. You're a fine girl anyway.'

Hondorp smiled with joy at the success of the game, and began looking forward to the other joy Elaine would provide. Since his first night with her, he had enjoyed what were to him the more spiritual gifts of Hendricks, but the prospect of another session with Elaine was, he felt, a prerequisite to continued existence. Though this feeling had started at the airport when he saw Hendricks giving him the eye and saw that the eye was stiff with commanding authority, his need was more than the counter to that bold advance. Hondorp had become a minor master of the strategy 'Want not, be wanted', and though he enjoyed the power over Hendricks this strategy gave him at the airport, here at the table watching Elaine parley with his father, he knew there were grander strategies, ones which overrode the others as tanks do butterflies.

'What is your reaction,' his father was asking Elaine, 'to being a public figure?'

'I can,' she said sweetly, 'take it or leave it.'

Poppa Hondorp nodded, his lipoma bouncing slightly away from his head, as a consultant who disagreed with his colleague's diagnosis. 'I suppose you people develop your splendid equilibrium in the practice of your art. I've often noticed how much Herbert has learned about controlling his feelings. I envy you.'

'He'll be learning a lot more in the next few weeks.'

'Ah so?'

'What's that mean?' asked Hondorp.

'Wait and see,' she said, purring.

'Don't be an ass.'

'Darling,' reproached Poppa Hondorp, a gentleman of the old school.

'Well?' pursued Hondorp.

'Well, hon-heart,' said Elaine in a tone whose warmth caused Poppa Hondorp to blush. 'Nobody can sus-tain it fawever. Get it?' Hondorp indicated coldly that he did not. 'I mean us golks are on top of the world now, but we can't stay there. Something's got to give, and when that happens, we're going to learn, all of us.'

'I understand now, Miss Parsons,' said Poppa Hondorp, his forehead losing the lines that had striped it when he had seen Elaine's tone in its true but to him incredible implications. 'Everything in the world changes, affections, infections, defections, resurrections, everything, and from every change one can derive knowledge, and at the end of knowledge is wisdom.'

'That is it, Doctor,' said Elaine heartily, and she reached over to pat Poppa Hondorp's hand. As if it were a game, he covered hers with his other hand.

'I wouldn't put it past her,' thought Hondorp, detecting in the spot of drool at the corner of his father's smile a reaction not unrelated to that which Elaine's tone and manner generated in him. After his portion of coconut and sliced orange had gone the disturbed route of the pot roast and potato pancakes, he announced that he and Elaine would forgo the evening in front of the machine extended to them by Poppa Hondorp.

'Big things in the air,' he said to his father.

'Don't show off,' said Elaine in her parodic manner.

'Let's go,' said Hondorp with threat in his voice, put there to excite rather than scare Elaine. The device served: she rose and thanked Poppa Hondorp for the lovely dinner.

Poppa Hondorp cast a quick look at his pocket watch, saw that the two minutes which intervened between Gleason and Caesar would go to the sponsors and so gallantly devoted them to praise of Elaine, dinner guests in general, and 'the art to which you and Herbert are giving yourselves'.

An hour or so later, at the hotel, after giving themselves to the first stage of a less recondite art, Elaine asked Hondorp whose side he was going to be on.

'What does that mean?' he asked feebly. He was flopped, arms straight back behind his head, feet tumbled on each other, barely energetic enough to relish Elaine's pressed fingers against his stomach. He vaguely hoped that the remark would not lead to some sexual refinement which might disable him for years.

'What we were talking about at your Daddy's house '

'Before or after your attempt on him?'

'Don't be an old prune now, Hondie. I mean the programme.'

'I don't get you then.'

Elaine lay back on him, reaching out her arms to cover his, capping his knees with the bent joints of her own, letting her head fall back so that her cheek was against his. After the adjustment, she said, 'I shouldn't care, I suppose. After all, whatever happens, there'll always be room for me, don't you think?'

Hondorp said he was sure of that.

'But I care for old Golkie in my way.'

'So?'

'Well, you don't need to be old Dunninger to understand what's going to happen to him.'

'What does one need to understand you? That's my problem,' said Hondorp, feeling a certain amount of strength coming back to him as Elaine lightly shifted her backside across him. He wrapped his arms around her and began a slow, complex massage.

'You've got it, Hondie,' she said, writhing in a still more complex massage of her own.

Almost entirely revived, Hondorp still held off long enough to ask what was going to happen to 'old Golkie'. The answer, however, was lost to him as Elaine loosed a blast of passion that rocked him senseless till the grey morning hour when he staggered into a cab outside the hotel and, parrying the cabby's questions about his connection with Golk, the doorman's respectful salute, and the elevator man's request for a pass to the show, opened the apartment door and let himself into bed for a twelve-hour sleep.

CHAPTER SIX

I

BY the tenth week of the thirteen-week option run, Golk had received no word at all about the renewal of the contract. The programme itself was running smoothly—there were no further golks about national figures or situations—and its audience ratings were very high, although, of course, not what they were in the early weeks. The golks were old-style ones, and were made with Golk's usual care. A morning screening was held before each telecast, and Lurcher, as network inspector, took over Golk's armchair. (Golk himself didn't appear) and nodded at the conclusion to signify that no changes need be made. He never said a word about Golk's future, and Golk did not bother to ask him or anyone else.

It was bruited about town that Parisak had settled damage suits by Long and Castelvetro out of court, and that he had dissuaded the latter to keep his thugs off Golk. A contrary rumour was that Long and Castelvetro had paid the network a substantial sum to destroy the kinescopes of the programme. A third rumour was that Parisak had asked Castelvetro's hoods to 'get Golk', but that the latter had refused because his amiable appearance on the network had bolstered his status with the union. Parisak was known to have gone to Washington to talk to Dammer, and it was thought that he had promised to contribute to a smear campaign to dislodge Dammer's nemesis from his senatorial seat in return for release from the inquisitorial grip of the FCC. These rumours reached the golks through items in gossip columns and talk, not through the network where it was felt that such speculation was dangerous. (It was generally believed that Parisak not only had the entire building bugged, but that he'd had his engineers develop some sort of electro-encephalograph which registered the vibration of treasonable thoughts.)

The golks went about their jobs more or less relieved of the tension which the initial burst of publicity imposed on them, but relations were strained. Even as they tried to act in the old way with each other, the knowledge that their actions had been and were in small part still an object of curiosity to millions altered the actions and deformed the relationships and feelings which engendered them.

For Golk himself, the strain was a condition he regarded as a test, and one which he could survive better than those who were directly or indirectly responsible for it. He was busy still with articles and interviews—the foreign Press and intellectual quarterlies had taken him up—and with the planning and shooting of the golks, but the activity was like that of an unsuccessful candidate for the Presidency in that it had the tone of aftermath. Whatever feelings Golk had about restoring the programme to its brief and glorious position as a maker as well as recorder of history he kept to himself.

Now and then Golk felt that there were too many balls in the air and that if he had to keep flinging and catching them he would go off his rocker. In that tenth week he took off the first day he'd taken since he'd come to New York. The faces of the golks, the chairs, the rooms, the props, the objects which stood there as the by-products of his will seemed to him its incarceration. He was weary in a way he had never been before, not as the letdown after triumph or reaction to temporary disappointment or sickness, just weary of purposeful activity. He called Hendricks and Hondorp over to him and said, 'Run the store for me, will you? I'm taking the day for myself. I've got to think '

'So,' thought Hendricks. 'There are cracks in it after all.' 'O.K.,' she said aloud. 'You deserve a little time off.'

'Time off, nuts,' said Golk. 'Life doesn't have such a commodity for the serious,' but the response struck him himself as an old record. He had the sense that time was cluttered with his impatience, that he had spilled himself out for years and years and that there had to be an end to the spilling.

He got up without saying anything more and walked by them out of the studio. Elaine was having a soda in the Whelan's across the street, and for a moment his feelings bunched for a leap in that direction. He'd slept a few times with Elaine, and prized her for the special sensation supplied. In bed she exuded pleasure in a fashion so ancient and yet so marvellously fresh that the sensation of it was what he remembered more than the breathing fruit of her body. He thought of it as he watched her with a blob of strawberry ice-cream at her lips, and then he matched it against his present need and found no correspondence.

'What is it I want?' he wondered, and he walked down towards the river, and walking, found out part of what it was: motion itself, undirected, needless motion, unattachment.

It was the coolest day of the summer. Golk seemed to feel his brain, his whole apparatus of intellection, spine, body nerves, sense pockets, open, detached from the denuded sense of movement, weightless now of plans, worries, conceptions, just touched here and there with street forms, sun, breeze, the sidewalk at his soles. He walked to the Roosevelt Drive and leaned against the paling, looked across at the Queens factories, the fragile slab of the Secretariat Building, the cars moving in the Drive and the bridges across the river.

No detail stood out, and Golk was used to fixing on detail. The lives in each car, on each floor of each building merged for him now, and it was in becoming aware of the merger, the momentary abandonment of his outlook that he returned to it. 'I can't make it as a mystic,' he told himself; but the appetite for the general had worked in him, and since he'd given himself the day, he pursued it.

He walked to a garage on Second Avenue, took out his long blue Ford convertible, went up the Drive and then out into Long Island. He drove for nearly three hours in and out along the shore, past the Hamptons and then into the easternmost inlets. Past a stretch of flatlands, he saw a small beach, grey and miserable in the late afternoon light. A hut was built up against a small wharf at the end of which a man sat on a stool leaning towards the water into which he dangled a line at the end of a pole. It was a vignette in grey tones, and Golk's eye took it in with pleasure; he wished he'd brought a camera. He got out of the car and walked the hundred yards from the road to the wharf.

'How do you do?' said the man without turning around. 'What do you want?'

'Just to talk,' said Golk, and he got up on the wharf which shook at his weight as if it had been constructed for its present tenant alone and resented any extension of its usefulness. The man aimed at him a long angular head dangling from a mop of black hair. 'Fine,' he said. 'Talk away, but you'd better get off the wharf. Sit on the beach. My name's Farrow. David Farrow. Mean anything to you?'

'It's a nice name,' said Golk, 'but you don't look Egyptian to me.' He laughed, but, as usual, laughed alone. 'Mine's Sydney Pomeroy. Glad to know you.' The man nodded as Golk stepped off the wharf. 'Why should your name mean something to me?'

The man drew the line out of the water. There was an

unbaited hook at the end of it. 'It's the name of the last king of the Montauk. Died in 1785, an ancestor of mine. Spelled differently, but the same name.'

'You do look kind of Indian,' said Golk, discerning in the denims and corduroys a poise which struck him as more graceful than that of the usual Long Islander. 'I suppose you claim the Island,' he said.

'No,' said Farrow. 'Of course not. We sold out to the English. The Canarsie and Shinnecock were the only ones who ever made a fuss about claims.'

'You live in the place-names. That's not bad.'

'I'm not much Indian. I've got my real last name from some dog-foot of Lord Howe's. It's Percival,' he added, beating the question.

'You lonely out here?' asked Golk. 'Where do you live?'

Farrow Percival nodded towards the hut. 'In the chateau there. I got a room in Long Island City too. What's your business?'

The bright drops of water slid off the fishing line and Golk thought of the crowns they made when a slow-motion camera caught them hitting the surface. Farrow asked him again, and he said, 'I'm a toy salesman.'

Farrow put his line back in the water. 'Dull?'

'Yes,' said Golk. 'The very word.' A pale spear of moon touched the edge of the sea and Golk took it in as balm. 'It's a real place you got here.'

'On the nights it doesn't rain or freeze. I got a heater for the cold, and an eight-year back file of *Life* magazines in there for the rain. I read astronomy books too.'

Golk asked him why he didn't use bait.

He turned around again, eyes lit up, and said that he was waiting for a fish dumb, mean, or hungry enough to take the hook plain. Golk's eyes lit with corrresponding flame. 'I get that,' he said. 'Have you ever found one?'

'Two dead catfish in the same week four or five years ago. Then I got a woman's shoe, and a lot of weed.'

'What more can a man want?' asked Golk.

'Supper,' said Farrow. 'If you want some, you can drive down the road about half a mile and bring back a few hot dogs.' Farrow reached into his pants and got out two quarters and a dime.

Golk took them and said that he'd be right back. He was back ten minutes later. Farrow had a fire going on the beach and they roasted the hot dogs. Golk lay on the sand and looked up at the largest stretch of sky he'd ever contemplated. Staring, he felt a kind of chill rolling in the stretch, an eeriness in the million points of star that, with the rest of what he'd felt since he'd left the office, turned him from his usual to metaphysical concerns.

'What's it all about?' he said.

'Who gives a shit?' said Farrow, flipping their garbage into the Atlantic.

'I suppose a man can't live out here alone and think too much about it,' said Golk. 'He'd flush his marbles.'

'I'm only out here summer week-ends,' said Farrow. 'And I read astronomy. That's enough for me. Knowing the names and the mechanisms which line them up there does me. I'm self-educated.'

'Me too,' said Golk.

'And I know my limits,' said Farrow. 'I don't bite at bare hooks. The view and the names are enough for me.'

'I suppose they should do me too,' said Golk. 'Though I don't even know the names. Except I might be able to pick the Big Dipper out of the mess.'

'That's not much,' said Farrow. Golk was flat on the chilling sand, eyes closed, face blank. 'Toy salesman,' thought Farrow. 'Ought to throw him in.' But, in an hour, he shook Golk awake.

'Thanks,' muttered Golk. He brushed himself off and said he might be back now and then during the summer; he liked it out here.

'Suit yourself,' said Farrow, and went into the house before Golk turned his engine over.

II

After Golk left the office, Hondorp and Hendricks looked at each other bubbling, as if a cork had been pulled out of them.

'Shall we do a scene?' asked Hondorp with an irony that pointed to the emptiness of the release now that the moment of bubbling freedom was past.

'Let's get out of here.'

'Lurcher wants to go over personnel matters with us.'

'Monday,' said Hendricks emphatically. 'Let's take a whole week-end off like human beings.'

'I'll leave word with Elaine,' said Hondorp, seeing her come in from her soda.

'Coward,' muttered Hendricks.

Hondorp followed Elaine into Golk's ante-room, leaned over and kissed her as she sat down and announced that he and Hendricks were off for the day, 'for the week-end, as a matter from fact.'

'With cameramen?' asked Elaine equably. 'Oh no? Well, come see me when you get tired of the staple fare.'

Hondorp told her to observe her place or he'd stick an apple in her mouth and send her down to Alabama roasted. Then he put a hand on her breast, and as it were, shook it good-bye. Elaine smiled peacefully.

Hendricks, who had observed this body play with disgust,

took Hondorp off by the arm. 'What an act you spider monkeys put on.'

'She relaxes me,' said Hondorp. 'She's about ninety-eight per cent c —, a rare phenomenon in the city. Among amateurs. It's like going to a Turkish bath.'

'Thank God you didn't start learning before you were half-dead, lover. Women would have to stay off the streets of the city.' But her words were lighter than she felt, and her mouth twisted into her cheeks with anger.

'There's Golk,' said Hondorp down in the street, and he pointed towards the river where Golk, an ambulant, inverted pear, was walking towards the paling, his great head like an Eastern dome over the street. 'Let's get a cab.'

'Ruddy coward,' said Hendricks, climbing in and giving the driver the address of her garage.

'Not Watch Hill again,' said Hondorp.

'We'll see. Grandmother would be so glad to see you.'

'I ought to break your head right open.'

'You are a brave one,' said Hendricks, feeling the old battle cries calling inside her.

They got out of the Bugatti, and then drove up Park Avenue. At a stoplight they looked into each other's eyes. 'Where?' asked Hendricks. Hondorp felt a new aimlessness in himself, one entirely unrelated to that of the undesigned walks of his former life, an aimlessness that was an evasion of destination.

'Let's fly to Paris,' said Hendricks.

Hondorp smiled. 'I don't have a passport.'

A taxi honked them into motion; they turned left around the gardened middle of the Avenue and started back down south. As they made the turn, the careless velleity turned desire in both of them. 'Let's go,' said Hendricks. 'I've got an International Air Travel card. We'll let the Greek pay for it. All we have to get is the passport.'

'That's all.'

'I wonder if there's a chance. Call up the Passport Bureau. Tell them your sister's had an emergency operation in a hospital over there, and you have to get to see her. It'll be like a golk.' There was a phone in the glove compartment. As he recalled this, Hondorp caught fire. 'Live your golk,' he said like an announcer. Hendricks turned again at Fiftieth and parked in front of the Ambassador.

It took four hikes up the bureaucratic hierarchy to get Hondorp's emergency to the proper level. 'I have to go to Paris for a day or two tonight,' he said in a voice compounded of urgency and command. 'I've never had or applied for a passport before.'

'Impossible,' came a soft contralto.

'My sister's having an emergency operation and the doctor at the hospital—the American hospital I believe— said it might be fatal. She's all alone, and I must go over.' He identified himself, gave references at the network, dug up his army serial number, and then waited.

The contralto returned, softer than before, and said, 'You can get an emergency pass good for two days with one two-day renewal. You may come down here immediately upon securing passage.'

'I'll be down in an hour,' said Hondorp.

'O.K.,' said Hendricks, far more calmly than Hondorp felt was warranted by the triumph. 'Of course,' he thought, 'for the rich and powerful, such a trip means nothing, but still, she must know what it means to me.'

'I'll go get the tickets,' said Hendricks, 'and I'll phone you confirmation at the Bureau.'

'All right,' he said, emulating her businesslike control. 'I'll pack a little and then shoot down to the Bureau.'

'We're on our way,' she said, almost mournfully.

They were, on a TWA flight leaving from Idlewild in

three hours. Hondorp had signed affidavits attesting to the emergency, rushed out to get his pictures taken, got back just before the Bureau closed, picked up his papers, taxied up to the Ambassador, drove out in the Bugatti with Hendricks, and they were off. The rapid and devious ease of the execution of what was for Hondorp a fantastic scheme drove him to an exultation equivalent to that he found in love-making, but as the fantasy was indulged, as the flight became less the means of slaking desire and more the realization of a fabricated need, it became a kind of nightmare for him. He had visions of his story being challenged at Orly, of telephone calls to Paris hospitals, of the discovery that he had no sister, of being landed in the Azores and left for days, passportless, stateless, waiting to qualify for the Azores' American entry quota. He left his filet mignon—cooked to a turn at Chambord—untouched on his plate.

Hendricks ate it after finishing her own. 'Why don't we do this more often?' she asked him. Her appetite for experience was revived by what left Hondorp hanging from his fears, the pursuit of novelty for its own sake, and she faced France like a college junior.

At Orly, Hondorp had some trouble with his papers, but his air of hush-hush (he didn't mention his sister), and a faked call to Paris hastened the inspection. He and Hendricks taxied to Paris, were driven to the Meurice, and asked for the best adjoining rooms in the hotel. They were assigned two fuliginous dens on the wrong side, but it was all they needed.

It was only as he was writing in his name, citizenship, New York address and occupation on the hotel *affiche* that he came to the full realization of where he was, where he had been the day before, and where he would be in two more days. 'It doesn't matter where you are as long as it's home,' Poppa Hondorp used to say, patting the largest piece of

furniture within reach, 'And this is home.' This pronouncement had filled blanks in Hondorp until his talk
with Hendricks on the terrace his first day as a golk. Now he
knew that it had served because he had never had the sense
of place. Today, riding up the rue de Rivoli to the hotel, he
felt that he was in the most self-conscious place in the world,
a place that demanded that you become conscious of it, of
its unlikeness to any place that you'd been, a place that
demanded that your life be shaped by, in, or against it. 'The
real thing,' Hondorp thought as he put down the pen. 'No
golk. The real thing. I'm here.' He wanted to start seeing
as much of the city as they could cover in a few hours.

This was not Hendricks's intention. 'The idea,' she told
him when he came into her room, 'is to see nothing, one or
two places maybe, exactly as we would if we came here every
other week, just for a good cup of coffee or to see a special
exhibit.'

'You're right,' said Hondorp, on the road to this convic-
tion, but more slowly than his admission. It was certainly
the grand style. 'I was on the verge of suggesting a bus tour.'

'That's possible, but the hell with it.'

'What places then?'

'Doesn't matter. We'll walk till we find them, or till we
get tired of walking.' They went out, and she pointed
towards the Tour Eiffel. 'You might as well acknowledge
the landmarks.'

'I saw that from the plane. Any others to hand?'

She waved towards the Louvre and identified it. 'O.K.?'

'Sated,' he said, though his heart pumped like an infant's
at his bottle. If he had dared, he would have said, 'Oh, the
wonder of life.'

They walked towards Concorde, Hondorp studying
Sulka's, the Continental, the bookstores and perfumeries in
the fashion of his New York *Wanderjahren*. The French

sounds and looks and smells touched him like a brook bath in the heat. 'I'm ecstatic,' he said.

'I'm glad,' said Hendricks, and she took his arm, *à la famille*. 'That makes monotony worth while.'

'Relax, Jeanine,' he said to her between looks, and warmly.

'All right,' she said sweetly, and found herself at ease. They were at Concorde, and the view of the great Place aswarm with cars, yet still open, sunny, capacious, ready for anything, guillotine or assembly, bowled them both over. 'Flip, flop,' said Hondorp. And Hendricks pressed his arm. something she had never done to anyone in her life. 'Like honeymooners,' she said to herself, but she held on wondering if the gestures of simplicity would bring in the feelings too.

This was the highpoint. A flock of jets curved maniacally over and away, and they turned melancholy. They walked across the bridge, down the left bank, and into a café at Quai Anatole France. They drank Pernod till their melancholy stiffened and they could lift it from them. They ate spectacularly at La Kermesse, then walked back up the river, across to Rond Point and drank whisky. Then they jumped into a taxi, went home and into Hondorp's bed. 'So I've had it,' thought Hondorp as he slid off to sleep, a Genghis Khan of life come late but fully into his own.

The next day Hendricks spent a year's golk income on the rue St Honoré. At Balenciaga's she bought three dresses without trying them on, this after a fierce fight with two fitters and a model. Hats, gloves, purses, underwear, shoes, she ripped the streets as if death were behind her. Finally she nearly catapulted a *bouquiniste* into the Seine by handing him sixty thousand francs for his whole stall of books and prints. 'Bring it to the Meurice,' she told him. '*Je suis le Plan Marshall.*'

153

Hondorp's only luxury was telephoning his father. It took half an hour to get the call through, and he waited in his room sweating with anticipation.

'Hello Poppa,' he said when the phone was answered.

'What's going on, darling? Where are you? Where did you spend the night? Why does the operator have to talk to me? This sounds like long-distance. Are you in trouble? Don't give me evasions. Come right back home.'

Hondorp waited under the cascade, and when it stopped tumbling said that he was calling for a surprise. 'I'm in Paris, Poppa.'

A sound like a discharge of birdshot came across the Atlantic. Then, ' "I'm in Paris, Poppa." You're in Poppa, Paris. What gives here on this phone? Whaaaat are you, Herbert Federn Hondorp, doing? Off the nut? This I ask you.'

Hondorp administered the final blow. 'I'll be back tomorrow morning. If you have a late breakfast, I'll eat at home with you.'

There was a costly, twenty-second pause, then a garbled proclamation. 'We don't wait breakfast for nobody *bei* Hondorp. Be here at eight.' The phone clicked.

'It was worth double,' thought Hondorp, and then noticed that he hadn't even used up the three minutes. 'But who counts?' he said aloud remembering a favourite joke of his father's.

That last night, they went to Ferdie's on rue Seine and listened to a Greco imitator do a Portuguese weep-song to a rock-and-roll beat. At the next table, a French hipster gave the eye to Hendricks, then jerked a thumb towards the Greco type: 'But it is the cheeck, no cat? *Fraîche*, no?'

Hendricks illumined the brazier in her eyes and nodded. The hipster started to turn his chair into their table. Hondorp, suddenly oblivious of his old fear of body contact, held up his hand to stop the traffic. '*Nous ne desirons rien*,' he said firmly.

The hipster's face contorted for an interpreting minute, then, having interpreted correctly, returned to his beer.

Hendricks opened her mouth and put it over Hondorp's. 'My great mannie,' she said. 'My Hondorp.' She laced fingers with him. Two teen-agers gone romping through dreams of contact, they swayed to the dark fandangos of the *cave*.

'So romancy,' whispered Hendricks. 'I've never had no real romancy.'

'*Pauvre chat*,' cried Hondorp. He was feeling his way, knowing no terms that would suit it now. 'It passed me by too. Just as if they hadn't invented it yet.'

'That's it, my Hondie,' she said, lips on his ear, inhaling from there, causing him to sweat. 'We're pre-Romancy. Stranded in the provinces.'

'Yes,' he said, 'yes,' unable to force out more but unwilling to break the continuity which was, he knew, promising a fine night. And more.

'Let's skip,' she said, her face tense with need. 'I so want it, even want you.' This whispered.

He moved clumsily upstairs, hand in his pocket to restrain himself. They couldn't find a taxi or the Metro station.

'Must one walk?' he asked.

Hendricks led him down streets to a ratty little hotel. St Thomas d'Aquin et l'Univers, put three thousand francs on the counter, secured a key, and walked him up two flights.

They came together, redeeming a measure of their loneliness.

The next day they flew back. For most of the ten hours, their hands were laced together. And even each other's handsweat pleased them.

III

An hour after the taxi brought them to the Parisak Building, Hendricks and Hondorp sat with Lurcher in a small oval waiting-room on the penthouse. They had been waiting ten minutes, minutes which the first two used to debate the reasons for the astonishing summons. The modest waiting-room was the sanctum sanctorum of the network, the demure hole in the wall where the honorary Doctor of Laws (Purdue '48) and Letters (Franklin and Marshall '51) directed the enterprises of which the network was but the most conspicuous. It was Lurcher's fifth or sixth visit to the office, but the others had never been higher than the eighteenth-floor observation tower (a pass was needed to get beyond that). They had, however, seen Parisak's helicopter descend and take off to and from the penthouse terrace.

'The standard wait is ten minutes,' said Lurcher. 'To let you compose your thoughts.' His melon head was seamed with wrinkles each of which was now a canal of perspiration. Still, he managed to sound calm, which annoyed Hendricks no end. 'Time to prepare one's case, but not time enough to get nervous.' She snorted, and the canals overflowed to make oases on Lurcher's flannels. Hendricks was gratified; she contrived a belch and took pleasure in another inundation of the canals.

'And you've no idea?' asked Hondorp.

'I never said that. I said I didn't know what was going to be done or said. It's clear what the cause here is.'

'Then why not call Golk?'

'Dr Parisak dislikes scenes. Golk makes scenes.'

'How would you know?' put in Hendricks. 'Have you ever caused one?'

'Of course not,' said Lurcher, and his eyes widened as

the door opened and a small man in the general shape of an Idaho potato on rollers appeared and said, 'Won't you please come in? I'm Dr Parisak.'

'Don't you have a secretary?' asked Hendricks, letting her surprise take the form of a question so that she could establish a position.

'Not really,' said Parisak leading them into a deskless room furnished à la Scandinavian, modern but with a bodied quality which came from three or four overstuffed chairs and a fifteen-foot sofa in front of an equal expanse of glass. The sun filtered in delicately; the room was cool, anonymous. 'I'm a guinea pig for the automatic devices. For instance, if you'll tell me what you'd like to drink, you'll see. Gin and quinine? It's that sort of day.'

Everyone said 'Please,' and four frosted glasses came out of the wall on a tray, were dropped easily on to tables beside each of the four occupied chairs. Hondorp noticed that the tables neither had legs nor were visibly suspended from the ceiling.

'Very clever,' said Hendricks, pointing to this same phenomenon and then indicating the manner of service. 'You must be very happy here.'

'I've heard you were a wit, Mrs Hendricks. It's a pleasure to enjoy you in person.' A cigarette box passed itself around the room. Hondorp laughed, or at least rumbled with the bubbling groan that served to release the energy which in others was called laughter.

Parisak looked at him, concerned, apparently found reassurance, and then said that some people felt that such antics were carrying automation too far. Lurcher said quickly that he didn't think so.

'Did you know that machines can reproduce now?' asked Parisak.

'How did you hear that I was a wit?' put in Hendricks as Parisak's question went unanswered.

'I'm afraid I missed that,' said Parisak, a shadow seeming to touch his face.

Hendricks repeated it, and Parisak said, 'I am acquainted with your former husband.'

They got down to business.

Parisak stroked his hard tan face with a hard tan finger, then removed it and said, 'Golk got us into trouble. He has no tact, only what I suppose you would call great gifts. We should like to continue to use those gifts, or at least the creations of those gifts, but we cannot use Golk. We want to continue the old-style programme, much as it's going now, but we want you two, Mr Hondorp and Mrs Hendricks, to supervise it. We cannot trust Golk's ambition or his tact. Perhaps we can employ him as advisory editor or in similar capacity. That is the only way the programme can continue. We want it to continue, and so do thirty-five million other people. It is one of our prestige programmes, and yet it is amusing. I myself think that it is one of the few real contributions to the medium. If you agree with me, nothing would give me greater pleasure than to take up the option with only the aforementioned alteration made. The programme is copyright by the network. There is no question of its being Golk's property.'

Hondorp felt called upon to say something, but was unable to. After fifteen wordless seconds, he heard Hendricks say, 'I should be delighted to help continue Golk's work. I think this would be in his interest as well as ours.' These words released in Hondorp a warm wave of acquiescence. He felt like laughing again, but, with some difficulty, held back. 'We've known,' he said finally, 'that Golk has been seriously overreaching himself. We've feared the consequences. This is more generous than we could have hoped for.'

'I'm glad,' said Parisak. 'Glad that you are able to speak

as it were for Golk himself. I had anticipated greater reluctance'—the shadow was again on his face—'but your breadth of vision is greatly appreciated, a great relief. Mr Lurcher will work out the details of the change, and will, as usual, attend your screenings in advance to see that they do not contain violations of the network code. This until you become entirely familiar with it yourselves.'

'I understand, Dr Parisak,' said Lurcher, formally, oddly, darkly. 'I only trust that Golk will.'

Parisak rose also. 'I hope so also,' he said. 'But at least the future of the programme does not depend on his understanding.' He took two steps forward, and then, almost like the cigarette box and the tray, he disappeared. They sat alone in the automatic room.

'Can we finish our drinks?' asked Hendricks.

'If you can swallow them,' said Lurcher.

Hendricks tipped up her glass and drained it. 'You're a surprise to me, Lurcher. Who would have thought that any feeling, bourgeois or otherwise, could survive in your sarcophagus of shit.'

Lurcher drew a handkerchief the size of a diaper from his pocket and drew it back and forth on his face. 'Poor old Golk,' he said.

For a moment Hondorp felt the same sympathy, and his feelings might have deepened except that the door they'd entered swung open and Lurcher said that this meant it was time to go. They went downstairs without exchanging another word.

IV

The Monday morning after his jaunt, Golk returned to an office whose foundations had shifted under him. He knew it the minute he stepped inside the room. People said 'Hello' to him as he passed their desks; orderliness pressed on things. 'You can't loosen the reins for a second,' he muttered, and he commandeered a screening, a Plans Meeting, a publicity run-through. Then, in his cave, he wrote memoranda on the budget, projected golks, thought of locations. The tempo accelerated, disorder crept back into the room, and he relaxed. He called Hondorp and Hendricks for a report on negotiations with the network; they weren't around. He called Lurcher; he was in conference. Golk was too busy now to mind a few obstacles to serenity; indeed, he needed disappointments to flag his work.

In the afternoon, he took Pegram out to shoot a golk, a scene in a butcher's with Golk passing off as steak what was obviously the hind quarters of a thin dog.

When he returned, Golk called up Hendricks at home and asked her to have dinner with him.

'I'm dead,' she said.

'What's the trouble? Lurcher giving you a hard time?'

That was it, she said, and said 'Good-bye.' Usually he was the one who introduced the matter of good-byes. It was annoying, if not worth a fuss. He rang up Elaine and she came over.

Elaine was always a joy to Golk. He had a Parisian twenties' love of the Negro and had primed himself for his love by years of reading *Ebony*, *Jet*, and *In the Dark*, even sending at times for the hair-straighteners and nose pins of their ads. Although Elaine's primitiveness was a contrived article—she was the daughter of a millionaire insurance man from Memphis and New York, and had spent half her life at the swish Negro resorts of the North-eastern states—he took to it as a source of power. He had discovered her at the studio where, as a seventeen-year-old, she was hired to dance for eight hours a day with fifteen other couples, a spectrum of New York races and types, the idea being that whenever a regular programme broke down, they would swing into rumbas. Golk took in one of the sessions, then worked out a scene using Elaine as focus, she being the only person in the room whose face was divorced from the mechanical Lethe of the dance. From then on, she worked with Golk, a splendid fulcrum for her weird revolt from the skin prison.

Golk's night with her almost restored his balance. But not quite. The next morning saw the same sluggishness, the same disquieting neatness in the office. It wore him down again. Part of it seemed to be that there were fewer people around. He dug out his personnel list and went over the names. 'Where's that cameraman with the salt-shaker nose?' he yelled from his office. 'Where's Gusberg?'

Elaine called in from the ante-room that Gusberg was out with Hondorp on some sort of deal.

'What's that mean?' shouted Golk. (There were no intercoms chez Golk.)

'*Une affaire de je ne sais quoi.*'

Golk shook his head in misery. There were no such affairs in his group. He called for a screening of yesterday's golk.

'Fitch is out too,' called Elaine.

'Golk me,' yelled Golk, not sure himself what that meant. 'Who asked for Fitch?' He flew out of the office, ran head-on into a teamster type pushing a camera out of the main room and asked him to set up a screening. 'I don't know how,' said the teamster.

'I don't even recognize you,' said Golk.

'Mr Hondorp told me to help out.'

'O.K.,' said Golk. 'I remember.' He reared back, let out an enormous kick at the camera muzzle, and fell back against a desk as the teamster pulled the camera out of range and wheeled it from the office.

Golk stared after him and set out for Lurcher's office. He was stopped in the ante-room by Lurcher's secretary who said that Lurcher was in conference.

'I'll wait.'

The secretary went into the main office and came out to say that Mr Lurcher's conferees had gone out the back way a few minutes ago.

Golk charged in. 'What's going on, I ask you? What's happened to my crew? Where's my renewal? Who's caring for me?'

Lurcher got out of his seat by pushing his hands on his desk, and came around to arrange a chair for Golk, led him, wide-eyed, to it, went back to his desk, took out a pint of Haig and Haig Pinch, tipped it for about four fingers, wiped his mouth on his shirt sleeve, groaned, and put it away.

Golk studied the actions. 'Not bad,' he said abstractly. 'Pudovkin couldn't have matched it. A mite like Ford in *My Darling Clementine*.'

Lurcher said quickly, 'We're not renewing, Sydney. You're great, too great for us, maybe too great for the medium. You've reached a point in your development where you can't and shouldn't be held back. We can't hold you. And we can't have you. Maybe the medium itself is too cramped for you. There aren't a million people in the country who can take you as you are now, and we live at the minimum of a million. Maybe this is too strong. There are a million of us who can take what you're doing and make it mean more to us than anything else we see, but the woods are so full of threats, of suits, we can't walk a foot without holding our breath. You can't live from day to day like that, Sydney.'

For Golk, Lurcher's words were suddenly visible, a mist around the repugnant continent where lived the world's beasts. Lurcher himself he hardly saw; the obesity seemed something abstract, eternal, the principle of opposition. He kept watching the words.

'We don't want to lose it all though. On Camera started here, it's still a great idea, and we want it—and you—to stay. We'll let Jeanine and Herbert handle the troublesome parts, and you can relax back and give them pointers, a grand old man of ideas. It'll be a vacation for you, and we'll see that you're not seriously abused on the mazooma side of it.'

It was then Golk lost the words and heard only sounds. These went on for quite a while, but he was looking through them at an ulcer growing in himself, a virulent emission of acids congregating in his body, and he had a view he had never before had, a look into the inner chamber of the world, the pulse of things, the principle of movement.

He threw up on the rug. Lurcher's head turned emerald; he pounded buzzers, gasped, opened his collar, and went to the sealed window as if it could admit air. The foul odours beat in Golk's head, and he rushed out of the office.

V

Golk looked at himself curled up in the silver ball of the Forty-sixth Street Automat's water spigot. He was all nose, mouth, and bald head, a worn-out ball in some occult soccer game. He kept staring until someone coughed him aside. Then he went over to a table with his glass of water and jelly doughnut, the last a treat reminiscent of the few he had allowed himself in his Providence years. Every two weeks, on his day off from the Boston Store, he had gone down to the docks, sat at a smutty restaurant called Button's Place, and eaten four jelly doughnuts and a cup of coffee.

Here he sat across from a tireless, coatless, fat-nosed blond errand boy (his packages on the floor and on one of the other chairs) gobbling blueberry pie *à la mode*. 'Seat's saved,' he lied to Golk, but dived back into his sweet gore when Golk sat down.

Inside and out, Golk was tired. On his walk up from the Parisak Building a massive woman had slammed up against him rounding a corner. 'Drunken bum,' she'd said as he bounced off the wall, for Golk was reeling up the streets, the hot weight of the buildings pressing on him, the sun grinding him, the cars on the avenues aiming at him.

Out loud, he said, 'What's it all come to?' His mouth was filled with dough and jelly, so the question came to little more than a groan.

'What you got to say?' inquired the errand boy, tilting an ant-eater chin towards Golk. 'Push it out of your teeth, man.'

'Drop dead,' said Golk abstractedly.

A fluid triangle opened up at the side of the boy's mouth. Blueberries whitened with vanilla cream edged down his chin. 'What was that?' he asked, eyes aglow with aggression.

'Shut your head or I'll punch it for you,' said Golk.

The boy's response to this was to grab the remaining half of Golk's jelly doughnut, push it into Golk's cheek and then rub it up and down his face. The sugared, jellied dough crawled in Golk's eyes and nostrils, all over his face and he sat there, stupefied, watching the boy grab his packages and shoot for the door with a valedictory obscenity. He sat, smeared and miserable for nearly a minute before dipping a napkin into his water and wiping off his face. 'I'll punch his damn head,' he muttered. 'I'll skin him,' but as he cleaned himself off, he couldn't even remember what the boy looked like, could hardly think where he was despite the sea of eyes, repelled, tickled, sympathetic, in which he felt himself floating.

He went out and walked up Broadway, losing himself in the moving crowd. He was in shirt sleeves, one side of his snap-bow tie hung down, and there were flecks of jelly on his collar. The great head bobbed back and forth, and from a distance he looked a loose buoy in the street. People circled him as he approached. Then, as he passed the Penny Arcade at Fifty-first, he saw himself in the window, saw himself as a stranger, a victim, someone to golk; he straightened his tie and brushed himself off. But the sun had touched him hard, his head was a cauldron, he dripped sweat on to his shirt, his underwear rolled up around his legs, his socks coiled his ankles. 'Lord God,' he said aloud, and people walking turned towards and then away from him.

He walked up to Columbus Circle and sat on a bench under the white column, rubbing a fist against his heart which seemed to him to be beating fiercely, irregularly. Sitting eased him. He sat legs out, palms open on them, eyes closed, breathing hard, pain entering and leaving him like trains at a bush station. He felt something hard in his right hand and looked up to a nickel and a fat back in a floozie's dress crossing the street. 'Ha, ha, ha, ha,' he went softly.

He squeezed the coin, and the contact brought him back, reorganized him. He walked down to the Nedick's on Fifty-seventh, drank four glasses of the orange drink, ate two hot dogs, and then took a cab back to the Parisak Building.

VI

The cloud, compact of puffed snow gleaming with the rising sun, Hondorp's future, that had been with Pizarro in the

165

bookstore, was overhead ready to discharge. It was inevitable, part of history's march, the forward motion of things, and his years of waiting were like the tranquil yawn of blue against which the cloud gleamed, white and promising.

Subcelestially, Hondorp told himself that Parisak's proposal was the salvation of Golk, or at least of everything that was important in Golk and which Golk in his artistically degenerate stage was trying to obliterate. Golk had been seized by that virus of ambition which so often attacks men of spirit: it consists in their dissatisfaction with what they do best, because the very ease of their accomplishment makes it seem a toy to them, illusion, make-believe. They yearn for the charisma of politicians whose hands can bring a city to tears or riot. Hondorp explained this to his father who now listened to his son's breakfast pronouncements with the gratified attention with which he himself used to be attended. More, he fed his boarder questions.

'But what will happen to your chief?'

'He'll be invited to act as advisory director, but what it'll come to will be his resignation. It's a business maxim'—Hondorp frequently took the stance of *un homme d'affaires* with his father—'that if they're too big to fire, just insult them. Resignation is the only sensible step he can take now. He should rest for a while, and then turn his talents—of which he has plenty—to something new. It's this turning in and about your own stuff which ruins you and it. Fresh fields and pastures new for Golk.'

The old man rubbed out a Hav-a-Tampa, a box of which was his son's bi-weekly gift, and sighed that man's lot was an inconstant one.

Hondorp, for whom life, up until a few months ago, had been a good deal more constant than not, said that Golk might well relish a taste of constancy, a routine which would let him take the world in, rather than having to supply it with his inventions. 'I've hardly begun in the supply end of things,' Hondorp said, holding up an index finger to drive it home for his father, 'but I'm already beginning to feel the strain of manufacturing. And this industry is worse than any other in the world. It gnaws away at your brain without giving it time to renew itself.'

'Come back home, sonny dear,' said Poppa Hondorp without a second's reflection, as if the remark had been stretched ready on an elastic for weeks. 'Why should more people than necessary waste their brains on the city riffraff?'

'It's too late, Poppa,' said his son. He was looking across the street at the cab stand to see if there was a free one to take him downtown. 'I'm in it up to the neck. I shouldn't even waste time regretting it. They don't want you to have time for that. That's the way they control you.'

This scene—of the great man's miseries—completed, Hondorp patted his father's shoulder, called 'Good-bye' to Marie, and scooted for the elevator.

In the splendid isolation of the taxi, Hondorp prepared himself for the confrontation with Golk. He and Hendricks were to meet in the office they'd been assigned by Lurcher on the tenth floor and then go in to Golk together. Hondorp did not look forward to it. Although he had rigorously excluded the word 'treachery' from all connexion with the supplanting of Golk, it lay in the soil of his anxiety. He would have to jump high to overlook so ugly a barrier to his succession.

In the elevator which had sped the three of them from Parisak's sanctum the other day, Lurcher had silenced the old nerve which had tingled sympathetically for Golk. He became then what he would be from then on, the *homo networkus purus*. 'All of us here are on the edge of going,' he had said then, 'balancing ourselves every minute over failures which would paralyse men in most fields. Where Golk's fallen, we can all fall.' When he turned reflective, his eye pips glistened, and were transformed into steel marbles, and the wires which held the great load of flesh together drew tight. (In contract discussions, Lurcher would relax, the flesh expanding as if in high tide.) 'Golk has become a commodity we cannot hold on our shelves.'

Hendricks, who provided a balance in every group by taking the role of the opponent, despite any personal contradictions involved, had aimed her head at Lurcher like a revolver muzzle. 'We're trafficking with a big man, Fats.'

Lurcher clutched at his midsection as if a genuine bullet reposed there, and after a gasp, said, 'An operating principle of executives in the entertainment industries is to keep shaking up the performers, so that even if the public can't tell the puppets from the masters, the puppets can.' The little eyes clicked around in orbit, and then they reported what was apparently stunned silence, Lurcher smiled. 'That goes for you too. Great opportunities, equal dangers. Smell of roses today, shit tomorrow. But we want you. You're the only people who can do the job. Now. Half an hour network time a week, and six hundred—apiece—until you make it something more. We're trying to sell some sponsors on the whitewashed version; it ain't easy, I'll tell you that. I'd advise you not to let your sketches include any sinister comments on vegetable oil or filtered cigarettes. Outside of that, you're free. No strings. None, that is, but the ones alluded to already. Now, I'm going to break it to Golk myself. Then you better have a talk with him. But don't let it affect you. If the surgeon sees the patient's tears, he's going to cause a lot more if he lets them make his hand tremble. Get it?'

'We get it,' said Hendricks, seeing herself, scalpel in hand, presiding over a lobotomy on the fat man.

VII

Poppa Hondorp's lipoma shared by now not a few of the characteristics of his head, and when Hendricks shook hands with him a few hours after their conference with Lurcher, she blinked to orient herself to the correct globe. It was the one which gulped and goggled at Hondorp's announcement, and which, after thirty seconds during which it seemed to stretch as if to swallow the whole room, levelled at Hendricks a question which responded to the announcement, 'So you're going to marry him? What for?'

They stood at the threshold of the living-room, and the lipoma twitched back towards the silent television set as a strayed child to its mother's cry. Poppa Hondorp, and then his guests, followed the cry into the room, and there Hendricks fixed her eyes on the soft veined feet which Poppa drew out of his backless slippers to rest on the table next to the *TV Guide*. Watching them was a relief from watching the monstrous anti-head on his neck.

'That's not the right thing to say, Poppa,' said Hondorp. 'It's not a proper question. In fact, it's an assertion.'

'You're not prepared for marriage, and you know it,' said the old man. 'And besides,' he added in a huge stage whisper, 'we're getting to be a regular hotel here with your friends.'

'Poppa,' growled his son.

'I've already learned how ready he is, Mr Hondorp,' said Hendricks, ignoring the whisper. 'At least, he's ready enough for me. Anyway, it's not going to be permanent. Don't worry about it.'

Poppa Hondorp was accustomed to the responses of television heroines, and he couldn't make sense of Hendricks's. Its strangeness, coupled with the substitution of

'Mr' for his proper title, smelled somewhat of a disaster, but he could do little more than inch ahead on his own thin path. 'Some are made for husbands, some for bachelors. My sonny is the bachelor type pure. Undiluted. For him, a woman permanently around the house would be like for me an elephant in the bathroom. It is not to the temperament.'

'He's bought me an engagement ring already,' said Hendricks. 'It's almost a legal matter.'

'With what has he bought?' This halfway between outrage and amazement. 'Let's see.'

Behind her back, Hendricks shifted a family sapphire from right to left hand, and held the latter up to the old man's proper head.

He sniffed at it. 'He's been stealing,' he mumbled. 'You've been stealing,' turning to his son.

'She lent me the money,' said Hondorp, batting his father back like a tennis ball.

The old man clapped his lipoma, sank back in his chair, and groaned, 'This world is not the world I know. I have no co-ordinate for this world. Where are traditions? Common sense?' He looked pathetically towards the silent screen. 'I should have guessed it would come to this. You don't break life open at the seams at the age of thirty-eight without festering.'

'Lovely, Poppa,' said Hondorp. The old man was getting tiresome, although Hendricks's clear relish of him upped his own tolerance-threshold.

'All right, enough,' said the old man, getting out of his armchair. 'I'll say no more but joyous things. Why dampen? I wish you both joy. We'll have a fine dinner, and then you two children'—he groaned here despite himself—'go out and enjoy yourself in the city, while I watch the world's misery in the Texaco news.'

'Time repairs everything, Poppa,' said his son with

gentleness, and he put an arm around his father's shoulders and helped him towards the dining-room. He had never before in his life made or felt like making such a gesture.

An hour later, he and Hendricks walked south on Central Park West, going back the same way on which they had made the connubial decision less than three hours earlier while sitting on one of the stone benches in the Theodore Roosevelt enclave of the Museum of Natural History. An hour before that Lurcher had called to say that he had told Golk of the change, and that Golk had taken it badly. 'Puked all over a twenty-eight-hundred-dollar carpet,' said Lurcher, this aspect of the *coup d'état* being the one he would remember longest. Putting the phone down, Hendricks had held out her hand, not particularly for Hondorp, but for someone. Hondorp had taken it.

'We'd better stick together for a while,' she'd said, and they went out and walked west and then north on Eighth Avenue. When they'd reached the museum, the sun was pouring a gold halo on Teddy's glasses and his horse's snout. 'Naturalist, Statesman, Author', said Hendricks reading some of the attributes incised on the white stone wall which ringed the briefly sanctified statue. They sat on the bench under the slab which read 'Naturalist', and looked over the green blur of the Park, holding hands like innocents fearfully *en route* to knowledge.

Hendricks was *en route* to what she thought of in Golk-like terms as a new form of knowledge. The concept, which Hondorp did not acknowledge, was the one she turned over and over in her own mind. Treason, the betrayal of Golk, was, in the long run, what she was, or so she thought, after. She entered into it not despite, but because of the special pain it caused. Feeling Hondorp's hand in hers, she said, as if prompted from the statue's heroic voice, 'The world was all before her.' The remark sprang from her lifelong devotion to the cult of experience. There was still something new to do and feel.

Just after she had left the boarding school in Vevey and had set up in the Hotel Louis le Grand off the rue de Rivoli, she determined, after the fashion of her Stendhalian heroine, that the next crucial step in her development was discovering whether sex was as important as girls of advanced stripe alleged. Her procedure had been simple. The night elevator man at the hotel was a dull-looking but well-built twenty-year-old. One night, Hendricks came home at three o'clock, woke him up, and invited him to her room. The young fellow's concern about his elevator was dissipated by a ten-thousand-franc note, and then, almost as effectively, by the sight of the young Hendricks's dress, slip, bra, pants, and naked body. Hendricks helped him unbutton his uniform, and then have, as it were, his way with her. A minute after it was over, she said, 'That will do. You can go back to the elevator.' She reached into her purse for another ten thousand francs, handed it to the grateful fellow, and turned in under her sheets. 'So that,' she'd said, 'is the great, distinguished thing.' For Hendricks, the distinguished thing was that its small charm had relieved her of what she knew would be the intolerable burdens of the chase.

Now she approached the betrayal of Golk with some of the same experimental inquisition. If the aftermath of betrayal was to be an uncontrollable depression, then the act would be worthless for her; if she was in control of it, however, the least new feeling would have satisfaction as an element of it, the satisfaction of achievement. Not that she was in such control of this experiment as she had been of the other, not could it be regarded—as that one was—as a trial run. One had to decide if one was going to risk it; she had decided instantly in Parisak's sanctum, her decision fuelled by Parisak's mention of her husband. Life was not war, for Hendricks, but war was part of life, and she had more training there than most. Now, as far as she could tell, betrayal would be no more significant than any other human relationship; still, it bore a history of fatality, and Hendricks was willing to risk the end for the feeling. Yet she wished to distribute her chances with someone else. And someone was at hand, and now, actually in hand. For someone who wished to manipulate his experience rather than be at the mercy of it, the coming confrontation with Golk promised a rare trial, and sitting in the declining sun next to her confederate, she relished it almost as much as she trusted that its aftermath would be the exultant feeling of further liberation from sentimentality. The anticipation of exultation filled the atmosphere she felt was appropriate to the dedication here in Teddy Roosevelt's Pavilion, the atmosphere of a brilliant, unmournful wake.

'. . . "where to choose their place of rest, and Providence their guide",' continued Hondorp. ' "They"—is it "hand in hand"?—' and he looked at her hand gripped round his.

'Shall we get married?' asked Hendricks. 'It will give people pause.'

Hondorp watched a pair of infant hoodlums scraping bird droppings off the backside of Roosevelt's charger and flicking them at each other. 'Legally?' he asked calmly, his verbal reaction outrunning his emotional one, which, when it caught up to the verbal calmness, fed on it.

'A detail. Living together publicly is the issue.'

'I'd like to, of course,' he said, the surety of the last revealing gaps in the certainty. 'The system of my needs has changed more than I would have believed.'

Hendricks laughed her rare laugh. 'Honey-dorp,' she said. 'Honey-dorp.'

'Don't laugh. What counts is underneath. I've been so used to things. There's such a lovely economy about tranquillity. And now it's been shaken and shaken. It can't ever be restored, but I keep wondering whether the new needs are authentic. Maybe they'll die out if I let them go.' His eyes were lost in the Park; he barely saw the enclosures of the avenues, the cars zipping up Central Park West. 'This park,' he said, 'used to hold all I needed.'

'Why reduce the world to your doll's house?' she asked, beginning in anger but modulating to sympathy and genuine wonder. 'Though maybe I don't have a right to say. For me, almost every year meant being freer and better. I had nothing really good to look back to. I didn't mind living in Watch Hill as a girl, but I've thought so much since about its damn dullness that I can't recover that; or certainly don't want to. My *parti pris* is for getting on.'

'That's a real doll's house to me,' he said. 'I don't even know why we're speculating like this about it. Speculating doesn't have very much to do with what we're going to decide, does it? I think I would like to live with you, have you around most of the time, sleep with you and talk to you. So let's say "Yes", more or less. O.K.?'

'This is my lust for novelty repaying me,' she said smiling. 'I guess you'll surprise me more than almost anybody.'

'Don't worry your future so much,' he said with an answering smile, and they linked fingers and looked, with their version of tenderness, into each other's faces. 'Shall we spring it on the old man?' he asked, and when she nodded, they walked up a few blocks to the house.

It was dark on their walk downtown after dinner, and in front of Roosevelt's prancer, and as a mockingly tender reminder of their partnership, they placed connubial kisses on each other's lips.

174

VIII

When Hendricks and Hondorp walked into Golk's cave like a tandem bicycle act, he looked up at them with a radiant kindness unlike any they had seen on his or any other face. It was as if a rock garden were transformed into a spring of flowers, sweet airs, and bird calls. It dazzled them. Lights seemed to play over the little cave as at a movie première. They stood blinking before his dagger-shaped desk waiting, penitents before the last judgment.

Golk had waited for them motionless for an hour, conjuring up the energy which was to illuminate their entrance. It was a spectacular display of artificial fireworks, one which derived from the coldest machinery on earth. So pure was the hatred which Golk felt, that he had, when the feeling was strongest, gone to the mirror to observe its shape, the lines it made in his face, the discoloration of the iris. The feeling had been strongest in the night of Lurcher's revelation. In the hours that succeeded, the hatred became almost abstract, divorced from the actions and forms of his old subordinates; and, in becoming abstract, Golk began to see it as a principle of behaviour. When they walked into the cave, Golk regarded them as vehicles of his feeling, and it was his feeling and what could be done with it that counted. He had a moment of surprise, merely recognizing them as people, these two whacked-up oddballs strayed into a universe of which they understood nothing. Nothing lasts, thought Golk, and feelings are the most precious transient of all. Only hermits like Farrow could preserve things, eight years of *Life* piled up in his hut. Not in the world, where action wore down everything, so that only in action did feelings or anything else count. So his smile was fixed by analysis.

'It's good of you to smile, Sydney,' said Hondorp, charging into the authority the smile seemed to assume. He sat on a corner of the desk, while Hendricks stood, held by that circumferential grin which had for her the glint of a web.

'I've always welcomed the inevitable,' said Golk, 'and been grateful when it hasn't beaten me to death. You two were more than I could have hoped for. If they'd have brought in some slick interviewer-type, I'd have shot myself, and maybe Parisak. I'm surprised they took it as well as they did. They're supplying all the counsel, putting up the money for any settlements, taking care of the publicity. Pretty decent. Of course, it had to come to this. I've known from the beginning. The idea was too good not to carry its own punishment with it. The sting in the tail —that's all. It was part of the enterprise.'

'Good show, Golk,' said Hendricks, using contempt as a veil for fear. 'Brave chap.'

'Ha, ha,' laughed Golk. 'I shall miss you, Jeanine.'

'Miss her?' asked Hondorp, determined to beef up Golk's smile, reduce its spread but give it solidity. 'Why miss her? You know everybody needs you here, and no one more than the two of us. That advisory job is not mere salve. If it's salve at all, it's for the wounds we anticipate having. The few notions we have all come from you. You let us fall and we bounce, but we can't bounce unless you let us fall.'

'That's a modest tack, Herbert,' said Golk gently. 'Very nice of you too.'

'You'd probably like to start something else on your own,' said Hendricks sitting down at the desk.

'That may be. I haven't really worried that bone yet. Let things come naturally. That's my tempo. I'll finish out the two weeks here, and then we'll see.'

'You know, Golk,' said Hendricks, and she took out a lip-stick and mirror. 'We're getting married.'

There was a short pause during which Golk's smile seeped almost all the way around his head. 'I should have known,' he said. 'Such collaboration as yours leads to marriage. I'm happy for you.'

'At least, we're going to be living together,' she went on, her vague hesitance that of someone translating a difficult text.

'I see. Of course, that's sensible. Nothing lasts. There's no reason for unnecessary—' pause—'systematizing.' He took a green cigarillo from his desk, flourished a kitchen match to flame, and puffed, the act becoming a kind of congratulatory fireworks.

'All good things seem to come at once,' said Hondorp, but sourly, as if he meant 'bad things'. 'And I suppose they'll go the same way.'

'Not unlikely,' said Golk with measured sadness. 'It's the wheel of fortune. On which I'm being racked a bit myself these days.'

Hendricks made the mocking sound of desperation usually represented as 'tsk, tsk'.

Golk's face seemed to shadow under the bright lights. 'Charming of you, Jeanine. I thought you'd been slammed into enough walls yourself to remember what it was like. You always did have a poison sac in you though, didn't you?'

'That's not like you, Sydney,' said Hondorp, doing a Sir Anthony Eden to the member of the opposition.

'And now look who's passing out the demerits,' said Golk, his eyes burrowing the green colours of the cigarillo, and glittering with the sharp turn of the discussion. 'The young Sammy, thirty-eight years of piety distributing its wisdom from its two months of contact with the world. What delicacy. What a charming turn of affairs.'

Hendricks was on her feet now, paler than Hondorp had ever seen her. Her face seemed the merest thickening of white light. 'The sword is drawn, eh Sydney? I'd wondered where it was. You're down in the dirt with us after all. You can't take it better than anyone else. Listen to all your victims now, pal. "Oh, the wheel of fortune racks me." You lousy little four-flusher. You were warned what was coming. We had it all out with you. That's more than your victims ever got from you, more than we ever got—advance notice. How great it is to see you feeling the squeeze for a change. This is what the world is for most of us. You've coasted through on nerve long enough. Vibrate, mister, vibrate.' She slapped the back of her right hand into her left palm, once, twice, and then rapidly; it was a miniature tribal dance of exorcism, all miniature but the wild flames in her eyes, flames which touched Golk's to equivalent incandescence.

'Head-on, eh Jeanine?' he returned, his voice lower than a growl, hoarse with contention and pain. 'The cesspool cover is off, eh? For weeks, you've been accumulating your stink, and now I see what it looks like. Why didn't I smell it earlier? You've been walking through this office like the plague, and I didn't see it till now. Look at you, the whiteness of the whale. You leper. And here,' with a long finger at Hondorp, 'here's the licker of your festers, drunk on your pus. You two, Judas and Mrs Judas. You lousy, four-flushing stinkers. What am I wasting my guts on you for?'

'All yellow now, eh Sydney? Backbone quivering, little lamb? Poor baby. All lost in the big woods. Hard world, lamby? Cold winds?' And her voice whirled from mockery into needling contempt. 'Wasted your guts on us? Why? I'll give it to you, rathead. Because we stripped our guts out on the floor for you to tramp on every day of the world. We were born giving and you came up grabbing and snatching and splitting. Now waste them. Waste them.'

Hands into the tornado, Hondorp groped ahead. 'Please, please. Sydney. Jeanine. What are we doing? Where are we going? No point to it. Break it off. Don't listen. It's just tension. We've had a hard week. *Doucement*. Things'll work out.'

As Hondorp talked, Golk's eyes yielded flames to embers and these to the familiar soft lights of his awareness. His bulk, which had swollen double during his outburst, had now retreated into his surprisingly petite frame. His hands folded, his great head bent over in shame. 'Awful. Awful,' he said. 'How awful. Dogs we were. Pigs. What did we say? What happened to us?'

Hendricks, panting in the middle of the cave, rocked her head up and down, back and forth all round on her neck like a fighter loosening up. She looked gone, lost. The aimless motion became the nod of negation, back and forth. 'Golkie. I'm sorry. Forgive me. It never happened.'

The cave seemed about to collapse with their shame. The three of them were still, sweating remembrance out of their systems.

'We can never be the same,' said Golk. 'But nothing can. Once you see the claws, you fear the scratch. Your own claws. Am I a wolf? Yes. I know it. In part. So what's to be done?' Inside himself, he heard the whirr of the machines. It was not unpleasant for him.

Hondorp and Hendricks regarded him as *aficionados* of a great artist might regard the one example of a late style. There seemed to be nothing else in the world but Golk, Golk and the winds and the bright lights, though outside, in the main room, they heard, but as if from another galaxy, the tiny cracks of a couple of typewriters. 'We'll go on,' said

Hondorp. 'Things won't be so bad. They'll work out. A few weeks will have us all through the crisis.'

'So he says,' said Golk softly. 'See here,' he said, and scrambling among the cigarillos, he came up with a thin glass tube of yellow pills separated from each other by cotton wedges. He held up the tube and the pills glistened; the tube seemed to be sweating. The sweat came from Golk's palm. 'Why not? I've got more than most, but I've done my bit. And what else? Nothing. I'm not much on food, on women'—a mournful look at Hendricks—'on narcotics. Why not?'

'Go ahead,' said Hendricks. 'If that's what's best. Go ahead. I'm with it. That's one thing we can do that the animals can't. End it when we want to.'

'Don't be nuts, Jeanine,' said Hondorp, and he clenched his fist as if to hit her in the face. 'What kind of stupid viciousness are you trying to peddle. The act is one for privacy anyhow. That's the most private of acts. Anything else is display, the worst.'

'Herbert knows he'll be an accessory,' smiled Golk.

'It's got nothing to do with that,' said Hondorp. 'Or very little. I'm not interfering with you, but I'll be damned if I'm going to push you off the cliff, or sell tickets while you go over. It's got about as much relationship to what you feel, as doing a buck-and-wing. It's like sinking into a marsh. The two of you don't give a man a foothold between you.' He shook his head, reached inside Golk's desk for a cigarillo, and then tried to take the pills out of Golk's hand on the way back.

Golk moved them out of his reach. 'Little Jesus Hondorp.'

'Quit laughing at your betters,' said Hendricks to Golk. 'A piece of decency left in this world and to you it looks like a turd.' This was said more in weariness than anger. They had all gone up and down the emotional roller coaster once and could not manage it again.

Golk reached for a bottle of Coca-Cola from inside the desk, opened it on a drawer, took one of the pills, swallowed it, and washed it down with a long swig of coke, a swig which was interrupted by his dropping the bottle to the floor and his head, with an immense crash, on the desk. This took about eight seconds.

A great moan came deep out of Hondorp. 'Ooghhhhhh.' He fell back against the wall of the cave. 'Poppa, poppa,' he moaned.

Hendricks, eyes bugged in unbelief, rocketed from paralysis, leaped up to Golk, pushed his head back against the chair rest, stuck her finger into his throat, elicited a tiny gurgle, lost him as he slumped over the chair on the floor, straddled his back, tried popping the head back again, then, her own head rocked back and she let his fall back on his arms.

Hondorp was down now, feeling for Golk's wrist. 'Where's the pulse? Where do you feel the pulse?' Failing to feel one, he rolled Golk over and put his ear to his chest. 'I think he's beating,' he said. 'He's still beating.'

'Golk,' said Hendricks quietly. 'Golk.'

'Pick up the phone,' said Hondorp. He sprang up to the desk, looked vainly for a phone, and then called out, 'Help,' but no sound came out of his throat. He started to run for the door, when he heard a small scream from Hendricks, turned around and saw Golk getting off the floor, brushing himself off, and smiling. From behind a corner light, the strange ship's head of Fitch poked out, the bow opened up dangerously, and the words, 'You're On Camera, kiddies,' came out.

Hondorp fell into Hendricks's arms. They put their

heads together as if hiding each other from Golk, Fitch, and the world. 'So,' said Hendricks. 'So you did it again.'

Hondorp was shaking, toe to scalp hair. 'Twice,' he managed to say, 'twice is too much.'

'Special event, my dears,' said Golk. 'Special event. Not for the show. Just a souvenir.'

'You're beyond belief, Golkie. Absolutely the end. How could you do it?' She was off the floor, making up at Golk's own mirror, behind which, of course, was one of the cameras.

'Don't we feel better, little one. Don't the juices run smoother. A little truth and a little shock never hurt anyone. Isn't this the road to health. And what a golk!' He was back at his desk, smiling, cleansed even from his abstraction. He had put it to work, had gone into action. He could start afresh. Before him, Hendricks and Hondorp stood like sheets on a laundry line, flying and crumpling in the high wind he supplied. 'Wouldn't have thought it, would you? Well, it's therapy, and more than that. Ever hear the story of the poet who came up to a young poet who was weeping his eyes out, complaining he was too unhappy to write. "Nonsense," said the old poet. "You've got a great opportunity right now, a whole emotion free to work with. You're exceptionally fortunate. A stone mason has to have the equilibrium of the stones he works with. That's all the emotion you're entitled to. Work it out, boy. Like the hot run and the cold swim, except at the end you've got something." '

'Such counsels he gives to us,' said Hondorp. 'Oh.' And shaking his head back and forth, a semaphore of depletion, he went out, and Hendricks with a tributary back glance at Golk, followed him.

'So there they go,' said Golk to Fitch, who was packing

away a camera behind a flap of the cave. 'My successors. The epigones.'

'What's that?' asked Fitch.

'The water after you've washed your socks and underwear in it for a week. Stick with them, Fitch. You'll get no more money from me.'

'Don't I know it,' said Fitch, and his mouth creased in a short smile, the equivalent in his face of all the lights in a mansion turning on at once.

CHAPTER SEVEN

THE night after the last golk made under Golk's supervision, Hendricks and Hondorp gave a party in the apartment which they'd bought on Sutton Place South. After they had signed the joint ownership papers, Hendricks had said, 'When we break up, I'll buy your half and you can go back to your father's.'

'I don't believe we should calculate such possibilities so early in the game,' said Hondorp. 'I look forward to many years on Sutton Place.'

To her surprise, Hendricks felt the same way. She regarded Hondorp and herself as somewhat unbalanced types who needed the equilibrium, however dubious, each other's unbalance supplied. 'At least,' she said, 'we'll be one arrangement of this sort where we won't pretend to be greater than the sum of our parts. So perhaps it'll last a lot longer than most marriages.'

'Many marriages.'

'All right,' she said, yielding to the equilibrium of rationality.

They even discussed the possibility of having children. Seriously, if briefly. 'I learned early I was my own child,' said Hendricks. 'So are you, oddly enough. We've made ourselves much more than most people make their children. We'll see though. No sense in making more foreclosures than necessary. We'll see how it looks after a year or so, if it turns out that we can manage that length.'

'What would the point of children be?' asked Hondorp, strictly for information.

'The point of anything else, I suppose. Variety of experience. And there's a big human element there too. We're no monsters. I played with dolls as a kid. There's something wonderful about total dependence. And total authority. We might even get to feel something new.'

Hondorp kept it cool. 'New feelings at our age are the sign that the old ones haven't been properly developed.'

'Buster,' said Hendricks, about to say what surprised herself. 'I'm only twenty-three. You've got fifteen years on me.'

'Unbelievable,' he said. 'And untrue to boot. I've used up only about fifteen years of energy. You were played out at thirteen. Or at least we're about even.'

And they went on in like manner, until, as usual with them, the chloroform of the abstract, the unrelatedness of what they said to what they felt, subdued them and sent them off to sleep. Though as they came apart in bed, Hondorp went back to the matter of children. 'The golks are our offspring now. And they last longer than the professional wailers if we take care of them right.'

Hendricks was too sleepy to interpret 'professional wailers' as 'babies'; she just nodded, yawned, rolled over to her side of the bed, and drowsed away.

The party came a week later; it served as hail to the new and farewell to Golk (it was reported that he was taking a six months' leave of absence), and more than this, it was both the engagement and marriage party—if not ceremony—of the hosts.

Golk himself had the cameras on it. 'For our memory books,' he said. 'We'll give ourselves a golk. The honeymooners at the wedding breakfast.' He moved over the room and the gardened terrace signalling Pegram and Fitch to change lenses and positions, directing people to move left and right, towards or away from groups, Cecil B. DeMille at the Red Sea. 'Warming up for the movies,' he said. He was supposed to be casing the West Coast.

The golks took to cameras as to air; equipment constituted no impediment at all to their case. Indeed, they would have felt less easy without the recording paraphernalia. It made the odd occasion of departure and celebration seem normal. End of summer, end of era, end of Golk, but it was all right: it went into the cameras. You could look at it always; age would scarcely wither it.

Still, some of the inner group, Fitch, Klebba, Pegram, Elaine, were affected by the occasion, and reacted by being especially solicitous of Golk. What the precise nature of his reversal was, they didn't know, but that it was one, was clear to them. Their solicitude took the form of the speed and precision to which they responded to his directions. They scurried here and there, tilted towards the sun or each other, smiled, bent, played ungolklike but lovely charades with cigarettes, curtains, themselves. It meant for some frenzy, a fringe of nerves to the ostensibly uninhibited affair.

Lurcher, the company agent at the festivity, shared the feelings of the fringe. He shuttled between Golk and his successors with a gracelessness that perfectly represented his uneasiness. He looked from face to face, and saw in each the fingers of rebuke. Except for one face, an outside one, which he could not place at first, could not in fact even distinguish as it approached him. He held out his hand and introduced himself.

Poppa Hondorp responded in kind. 'I'm the father of the host, Ossip Hondorp, Doctor of Medicine.'

'An honour,' said Lurcher, falling into Poppa Hondorp's own manner. 'It's a relief to see someone from outside our barbarous little world.'

'That's understandable,' said Poppa Hondorp, a bit shakily. He was still getting his sea legs for this world beyond the locked rectangle of his routine, office, television set, dining-room, and bed. He confessed: 'For me, the adjustment is not easy.'

Lurcher found no response to this; anyway, he was remembering the unique head before him. 'I saw you on the programme,' burst out of him, and to Poppa Hondorp's large smile, he added a yet larger one.

'Over one hundred people have mentioned this to me,' said Poppa. 'I'm grateful for the acknowledgement. What was your opinion of the little vignette?'

'Charming,' said Lurcher. 'Totally charming. I only wish that the programme had continued to display like charms.' This with a backward look for possible auditors. There were none in range.

'I find it always engrossing,' said Poppa, not from loyalty, but as the simple revelation of his existence. 'And this even before my Herbert became a cog in it.'

'Engrossing, yes,' said Lurcher. 'I agree. Too engrossing perhaps. And this is a mighty rare remark for a network man like myself. That hoodlum, in fact, was so engrossed that for a while we kept expecting Golk's head to come floating down the East River.'

The remark was beyond Poppa Hondorp who had, firstly, made no distinctions between the golk victims, or at least none that would enable him to identify one as a hoodlum. The remark did strike Elaine, however. She had come up to take Poppa Hondorp's arm close in her own. The old man felt the rare and disconcerting sensation of a woman's body up against his own, and could barely stammer a greeting to what he finally managed to recognize as his old house guest.

'A pleasure here too, Doctor,' said Elaine, and she directed Poppa Hondorp's eyes to Fitch's camera which was boring in on him for a close-up. Poppa forgot the warmth creeping up his side in the contrivance of a benign, elder-statesman smile, which was scarcely disturbed by Elaine's gentle stroking of his lipoma. Poppa bowed his head, a lesson in private serenity for the American fellaheen.

Dr Parisak had sent over a case of Piper Heidsieck. It circulated now for toasts. Golk asked everyone to raise his glass towards the centre of the room, and there, in the steel streaks of sunlight, there was a twang of glitter as Golk called out—waving Fitch back for a medium shot—'Something borrowed, something blue. Ring out the old, ring in the new.' The toast was drunk with a variety of feeling.

'And to friend Golk,' cried Hendricks almost before the first swallow had passed the neck lines. 'Long may he prosper, and may he bring others to the prosperity to which he has brought us.'

There was less variety of reaction to this toast. 'And,' said Poppa Hondorp, his head filled with the two swigs of bubbly, 'if I may be so bold, an outsider, as it were, though a well-wisher, and even sometime participator, a toast to the young couple which here begins its joint life, in play and work, in office and bedchamber, in the harness of harmony.'

'Bravo,' called Golk, and he urged Fitch's camera on to the trembling auxiliary head, decked out in the late afternoon lights like a whore at a wedding.

Hendricks waved the servants—ones supplied by the network—around with the champagnes. Pegram flipped a glass back against a wall. 'Cheers for Old Nass,' he cried. (His education had extended to a year at DeWitt Clinton High School.)

'Cheers,' cried Klebba, and threw his own to shatter against a reproduction of the Embarkation for Cytherea. A rage of glasses followed, some not emptied of champagne and Scotch. Golk had Benson's camera covering the walls; he glittered with pleasure.

'Halt,' called Poppa Hondorp. 'Stop. What gives here? Immediately halt.' Hondorp breathed relief as his father's thunder subdued the riot. 'What are you doing to the newly-'—a short stumble—'weds' lovely house? We must contain ourselves.'

The glass-flinging ceased, to Hondorp's surprise if not to his father's. 'A toast to my dear father,' he called, raising one of the few glasses in the room that had stayed where it belonged. 'Without whom not.' There was a buzz of 'Hear, hears', and two or three lesser golks drank the toast. The others foraged for fresh glasses. Poppa Hondorp moved over to his son and put his arm around his shoulders. Tears were in his eyes, and his head dipped back and forth with its shadow of flesh till he found speech. '*Ein braver Bub, mein* Herbert,' he got out, and he wiped his eyes on his son's coat sleeve. Hondorp moved the sleeve around, patted his father on the back, and moved off. Enough was enough.

But Golk had not had enough. An orange flew under Hondorp's nose, and as he stepped back, a grapefruit brushed the fuzz at the back of his neck. The golks had found the fruit bowls and were tossing the contents back and forth across the room. 'Spring training,' called Golk, whirling Fitch and Benson in with the cameras. Apples, pears, peaches, plums, nectarines, grapes, and then a persimmon, which Klebba dodged and which splattered against an ivory wall. Poppa Hondorp folded up into an armchair, his arms clasped over his head, eyes wildly peeping out at the madness.

'Plomp,' cried Golk at the persimmons, and waved Fitch in for a close shot. Hendricks tossed with the rest, flinging like a man, cracking her wrist like a ballplayer. 'Zing,' she went, releasing a tangerine across the room to Gusberg, a spectacled string bean with St Vitus dance who scooped it off the back wall and lanced it back to her an inch over a Spode vase mooning on the sidelines.

Behind the piano crouched Lurcher, his head more conspicuously melonlike than ever. He had moved there when Pegram's hand had momentarily gripped his head as if around a particularly promising missile. 'I should never have come,' he told himself. 'I should have guessed how that bastard would explode, once he exploded.' His chin hit the piano as he ducked a banana which, instead, tore some paint out of a real Dubuffet hanging there, innocent.

The fruit-throwing stopped when a cantaloupe shattered a window on its way to the East Side Drive, followed four seconds later by an air-curdling shriek from the road. 'Sorry,' called Golk out between the fragments. 'It didn't even hit her,' he assured the others.

The tempo of the party changed. The golks slumped in sofas and chairs, holding out their glasses to be filled and barely talking. They drank for hours, long after Poppa Hondorp and Lurcher left, and finally all were prone, either in the sofas or on the floor, all but Hondorp and Golk who prowled among them like Henry V the night before Agincourt. Heads bent they walked around, until they met head-on over Hendricks's unconscious body, and looked up into each other's bleary faces. 'It's all yours, Herbert,' said Golk slowly, and with this he tensed. Hondorp sprang back, his face awake now and contorted with terror. Then Golk shook his head, and walked out of the apartment, slamming the door so hard that Hondorp, like Ugolino in the tower, heard the lock click shut.

A flag in a night breeze, Hondorp trembled for more than a minute. 'I ought to count up the dead,' he thought, 'including myself,' but instead, he went down the hall to his bedroom, flung himself on the bed, and slept. Hours later, when he rose, the apartment was completely empty. The maids had cleaned up the remains, and even the shattered window-pane had been replaced. If it hadn't been for his clothes, wrinkled about his body like an old man's skin, Hondorp would have had trouble believing that the party had taken place.

CHAPTER EIGHT

I

THE first letter arrived almost a year to the day after Golk disappeared. It was addressed to Mrs J. W. Hendricks, You're On Camera, The Parisak Building, New York, N.Y., and was marked 'Urgently Personal'. As soon as she picked up the envelope, before she'd remarked the handwriting, Hendricks felt that it was from Golk.

Not that there was any rational support for such feeling; she hadn't been thinking of him and he hadn't been heard from. Since she and Hondorp had taken over the programme, their lives had proceeded with an easy rapidity and an easier success. (In Klebba's view, what little success there was came from rifling Golk's files.) Melancholy reflections, guilty regrets, and nostalgia played no parts at all in them. Golk's disappearance caused but the slightest of shocks, and a few days after it was realized that his departure was in the nature of a disappearance, even this shock was dissipated in the swing of their lives.

About two weeks after the party, he had called in to say he was 'off for points West. Just going to scout my way around for a while,' and they had wished him luck. A week later they got a postcard from the Carlsbad Cavern Bat Caves. It went, 'The bats are all rabid. Just had vision of a great golk: honeymoon couple come to sightsee here, bitten by rabid bat, and, on camera, suffer hydrophobic agonies and perish. Best to you both, G.' Neither she nor Hondorp found the card either witty or macabre; in their view, it was but another of Golk's misplaced efforts, a combination of a sudden notion and a sudden pique. They forgot it, and soon forgot him. They stopped wondering at his not coming back and his not explaining this in letters. Now he was more like some story they had made up to explain the terminology of the programme. Golk's personality was buried under the load of verbs, nouns, and adjectives which bore his name.

The envelope which Hendricks slit open with her fore-finger nail was postmarked Puma, Arizona; the enclosed sheet of dime-store-pad paper bore no salutation. It went as follows:

> When I drove out of New York last year, a strange thing happened to me. I was following a 1953 Nash station wagon—the kind in which the back seats fold down into a bed—and was staring into the face of a young woman lying down. She had an unearthly expression of weary contempt on her face and I was intrigued by it. I kept close behind the car risking life and limb at various crossings. (It was on Rt. 20 in Ohio.) The car pulled into a driveway somewhere near the Indiana border, but so suddenly that I followed it up. Two uniformed men came out of the house, lifted the woman out of the seat on to a cart, covered her with a sheet, and wheeled her into the funeral parlour. Why not? G.

The next letter came a month later from Grandview, California. By that time, Hendricks and Hondorp were more or less prepared for it. This letter seemed more remote even than the first, which had, after all, some of the flavour of a personal experience. It went:

> You know Newton did nearly all his good thinking before he was thirty? For the next forty or fifty years of his life, he was more and more of a crackpot. He spent his time doing crazy calculations about the beginnings of the world (4004 B.C.) for instance. He believed that the

secrets of the universe were inscribed on a Babylonian tablet, and that he and a few other select brainworks were occasionally given peeps at it. Who knows? G.

After she'd read the letter, Hendricks took a sack of betel nuts out of her desk, chewed and spat out about a hundred of them. The floor was empurpled with stain, but today the nut binge did not relax her; indeed, after a while, there was an aggravation of the awareness that had been with her ever since she'd thrown the first letter into her waste-basket at home. The awareness transformed her bright new office into a kind of echo chamber, a sensorium, a huge nerve against which the most ordinary sounds, sights, and smells registered with painful force. Golk's new letter was a jabbing addition to this living palette. Hendricks let its phrases find their odd interior destinies inside her until they unleashed themselves from their origin and from meaning itself. Only when this happened did she feel free of the letter.

That night, though, at dinner, she went through the business with Hondorp. (To their own surprise, they were still together on Sutton Place.) 'What's going on with him?' she asked.

Hondorp lifted his head from a forkful of sherry-soaked crabmeat. 'I'm not sure, but I should guess that he's seen the show and hasn't liked it. He's letting us know that he thinks something's wrong and something else had better be done about it.'

Hendricks shook her head, partly at a silver dish of *petits pois* which a maid proffered, partly at Hondorp's analysis. 'What's Newton got to do with all that? Is Newton the programme, good for thirty years, afterwards lousy, or what?'

Hondorp mumbled through a mouth of crab that the contents were irrelevant. 'He's just making us a sign.'

Hendricks puffed smoke across the rim of a glass of Pouilly. 'I'd like to know the answer to one question: Is he with us or against us? Is he pushing us towards the cliffs or driving us away from them?'

Hondorp crooked a finger at the maid for dessert. 'Maybe he's trying a kind of long-range golk on us, exerting pressure via letter to see if it'll show up on the programme. At any rate, he's trying to work out some sort of contact with us again, maybe out of loneliness, maybe out of regrets, maybe out of genuine affection for us or the programme. It's the latter possibility which works on me. If he's concerned about the quality of the product, he's got a real case. We've been turning out one hell of a product.' They looked sharply at each other, half to accuse, half to ward off accusation.

Hendricks pushed away her dessert and got up, her face knotted with disgust. 'The whole business is played out. We know it. The network knows it. Everybody but the damn audience knows it, and it's catching on. We're boring the bejesus out of everybody, especially us. If it weren't for the damn shekels, I'd never set foot in the place again.'

'What we need is rehabilitation,' said Hondorp, and he spooned up a brown hill of mousse as if for illustration. 'New air, maybe new lungs. It's going to be hard, but our lives are on it.' The mousse was gone, and his finger waved for cheese.

Hendricks was at the window looking out at almost the same view of the Queensborough Bridge that she saw from her office. The slight displacement of this evening view gave her an odd feeling, as if the two parts of her life, the night and day parts, were trying to be connected but weren't. 'Or are they like the different foci of the eyes?' she thought now, staring out at the river, a silver band binding in the island. 'To get dimension,' she said out loud.

'What?' asked Hondorp, gobbling a lump of Camembert from a milk cracker.

The blooming plants on the terrace outside were losing their thrust and scent and colour. 'What are we going to do?' she asked.

Hondorp lit up a sleek Cuban cigar 'Made in Havana for H. Hondorp'. 'I've been knocking it around for a couple of weeks,' he said. 'One thing I know is this: we've been too constrained, too bound in. I want to get out in the *belle étoile*. I want crowd scenes, a sense of place. And New York isn't the be-and-end-all of creation either. We'll move around the country, Missoula, Montana, Coral Gables, Florida, Puma, Arizona. Who knows? Maybe even Caracas and Marseilles. We'll live it up.'

'You think moving around solves everything. That's standard stuff,' she said. 'And it never works. When a programme is leaking, you don't solve matters by trying to race it around the globe. You just leak faster. What we're gripped by is something like gravity, something unsolvable.'

Hondorp slammed a palm on the upholstered arm of his chair. 'Missiles,' he said. 'Get the right propulsion and you lick gravity. I know it's hard, but it's possible. Take that damn film of our party. A pain in the neck, but it was a new feeling, a new type of thing. Very refreshing. It was the use of a crowd, a group. We can work with that for a while.'

'Perhaps,' she said, distantly, as if neither this nor anything else concerned her any longer.

Hondorp stared at her, long, blonde, and familiar, looking, against the windows, like bizarre, marvellous drapery. 'We're at the hot gates,' he said. 'We don't have time to fold up. Don't let the letters get you down. I know they're like dirt knocking into your coffin, but we can't let him bury us.'

'Metaphors,' she said.

Hondorp got up and went into his study. His exits almost always prevented their rounding the corner of disagreement into arguments and battles. It was the way they weathered those storms of temperament which years of intractability had stored up for encounters much milder than those they had on even their calmer days.

The study was three ten-foot walls of books—bought on one ecstatic trip to Follett's—a lounge, a Queen Anne desk with Florentine fittings, and a twenty-eight-inch television set controlled from any of the four armchairs by a switchboard built into the arms just beside pads and pencils. One could never tell when key thoughts would strike, and Hondorp was ready. Each night, he picked up the pad jottings, assembled and had them bound into red leather looseleaf books which were lined up on a special shelf close to his favourite chair.

Hondorp lay back on the couch, exhorted the chandelier above his head for assistance, and waited for it. By ten-thirty, it had come, and he had scribbled his 'Techniques of Rehabilitation for You're On Camera' down on a number of the pads, collected and reread them. He went into the bedroom where Hendricks, almost aglitter in a pale blue nightgown, lay in bed reading a book in a dark-blue dust jacket called *The Assistant*. 'Study in blue,' said Hondorp.

'This is some book,' said Hendricks.

'I've got it worked out,' said Hondorp, taking off his jacket.

'You're not much of a reader any more,' said Hendricks.

Hondorp took off his shirt, threw it over a chair, and topped it with his pants. 'I'm working in another art form,' he said. 'I'll get around to it.'

'You'll get around to nothing,' said Hendricks, turning over on her side, putting the book on a night table, and turning out her bed light. 'You broke the spell.' Naked,

Hondorp swept up the bed covers and lay next to her. 'Such a good part, too,' she said. 'Push off.'

He was enough occupied with his new plans not to care one way or another. He rolled over to the other side, snored a little to annoy her, and then went off to sleep. After a while, she put on the bed light and finished reading the novel.

II

The first golk in what could have been—but never was—called hondorpism was shot a month later in Comiskey Park during a Yankee-White Sox game. Four cameras were used, mostly for the panoramic placement which Hondorp felt was demanded by rehabilitation of the programme. There were shots of the parking lots, the stadium walls, the ticket sellers, the peanut vendors, the regular television cameras and the sportscasters, the sun against the flags, the dugouts and then faces in the crowd. 'I wish we had colour for it,' said Hondorp to Benson, who was carrying the audio equipment around in an ice-cream vendor's container and responding to requests for frost-sticks and Dixie cups by calling out 'Empty' every minute or two. Hondorp wandered around for a while almost as he had when he was a man of leisure, taking in the smoke-blue Chicago sky, the tender green field and the noise and colour of one of the few large crowds of the regular season. 'I'm going to put in for colour,' he said. 'It's like operating sails in a power age. We're not in this for the sport of it.'

The golk itself centred about the reactions of a group of Chicago fans to the game. No golks were planted: all were, in a sense, victims. The microphones were under the seats, and two cameras were fixed to iron pillars which framed the row. Another camera followed the game so that the reactions could be co-ordinated with the ups and downs on the field —'bringing in more of the world to golkdom' as Hondorp put it—and the fourth camera cruised with Pegram for background shots—'extra-dimensionality' was Hondorp's term for this in his jottings.

The editing turned out to be the big job, and back in New York the next day, Klebba and Hondorp began a back-breaking week of putting the footage into shape. There was a natural reversal to the scene, the ten minutes of the fourth inning during which the Yankees overcame the White Sox early lead, but that was it. The rest of the golk featured the increasing depression of the ten faces in the row. Hondorp tried to pad the mute drama with the background shots which would extend it into a sort of documentary of Base-ball in Chicago or American Spectator Sports, but the centre was soft and nothing really held on to it. The night before it was to be telecast, Hondorp wrote a humorous narrative to sew it together, and this helped somewhat, but as he and Hendricks watched it the next night (each on a different set in case of mechanical failure), they both saw ineptitude and failure leaking out of the screen.

They saw something else too. About three-quarters of the way through, each of them gasped, and then heard the other's gasp as a confirmatory echo.

'Was it really there?' asked Hendricks, the sounds fuelling more on intake than exhalation.

'Keep watching,' said Hondorp tensely, leaning forward as if proximity to the glass would conjure there the image he sought.

When the programme ended, they did not discuss its defects. Only the apparition in one of the back rows during a background shot of the crowd. 'It couldn't have been he,' said Hondorp. 'Why would he be at a baseball game? And in Chicago. A week ago he was in Arizona or someplace.'

'It was he,' said Hendricks dully. 'You could see him three or four seconds.' Towards the side of the frame the great skull had caught up the sunlight and focused the frame on itself. 'Everything in the scene seemed to be pointing to that auk's egg of his.'

'The baldness throws us,' said Hondorp. 'Bald men look alike. The way Chinamen do to Westerners. Or Westerners to Chinese,' he added in fairness.

'The shot wasn't the world's clearest,' she conceded. 'Not that any of the camera work was very good considering all the sun you had out there.'

Hondorp ignored the general criticism, and took to bed with him the problem of Golk's presence at the game. The next day he asked the golks at the office if they'd noticed anything peculiar. The inner circle thought they had seen Golk there, yet none of them but Elaine reacted to it more than they did to anything else in the universe, quotidian or miraculous. Facts were facts, and life itself was technics. Elaine, however, drew on disowned tribal memories of witchcraft for her account of it. 'That old sonovabitch is hexing us.' Hondorp reached a hand over to cradle a breast. 'Don't phutz around,' she said. 'We're in for it, and I'm no one to jitterbug at a funeral.'

The only critique of the show panned it as 'diffuse and pointless,' and pointed to a general weakening in the quality of the programme. The golks felt the same way about it. 'We're just starting,' said Hondorp in response. 'It'll take us a little while to bring this crowd stuff off,' but heart lagged behind words.

Two days later, they tried again, up in Groton, Connecticut, at the launching of a new atomic submarine. Klebba, in overalls and denim workshirt, tried to persuade a guard to let him up on the V.I.P. platform on the grounds that he'd helped build the sub. An argument started, abetted by a golk or two, and spread from the platform to the crowd surrounding it. Police took Klebba off where Hondorp waited with the release slip signed by the Commandant of the area who had not quite understood the nature of the 'television coverage'.

The editing job here was simpler, and the golk seemed much more successful than the first. In the preliminary screening, that is.

The night of the telecast, Hendricks and Hondorp again watched at home. Two minutes after the golk began, they saw the skull. It was up near the bald prow of the ship, at the fringe of the crowd, and for a moment, it looked as if there had been a double exposure of the picture, or as if another submarine had surfaced alongside the debutant. The skull gleamed in the background of three or four minutes of footage, and each time it appeared, Hondorp felt the structure of the programme collapse.

Neither he nor Hendricks said a word until it was over. Then Hondorp yelled, 'How could he know where we'd be?' He was amazed, frightened, and fiercely angry.

'Don't look at me,' said Hendricks. 'For my money, we're just seeing things.'

The next day, Hondorp ran the film through a scanner, slowed it at the proper frames, cut a couple out, and looked at them under an enlarger. A bald head, which might or might not have been Golk's, showed up. 'She's right,' said Hondorp to himself. 'We're seeing things.' But the inner circle of golks had seen it too. 'I'm heading off,' said Elaine, as Hondorp came back to his office. 'I've had it. I'm packing.'

Hondorp cut the air with a fierce look of contempt. 'Head off,' he said. 'You chicken spade.'

'Ha, ha,' she laughed unhappily. 'You're doomed, pally. I'm going to save what little of this distinguished skin is there to be saved. The programme's had it. Here,' and she tossed him an envelope with a gold 'P' on front and back.

Hondorp slammed the door, and read the memorandum. 'Your programme seems to be losing fire,' it went. 'I offer you this word as a reminder that no one can coast in the world of entertainment, or in any other for that matter. Entertainment must entertain. When it ceases to entertain, it must be replaced. Your Trendex and Hooper correspond in showing a 6 per cent drop from your last offering. This is the third consecutive drop for the programme. I wish you luck. P.'

That afternoon, another letter came, this time to Hondorp. It was postmarked Sioux Falls, Iowa, and had been mailed the day they had shot the scene in Groton. It went:

A professor in Iowa City the other day told me something I should have known years ago. 'Golk' is a real word, and he told me to look it up in this dictionary of all the English words. It's spelled a few different ways, but they all mean 'cuckoo' or 'fool'. For instance, the dictionary quotes a poem written three hundred years ago: 'Art thou a god? No—but a gok disguysit.' 'Gok' is one of the ways you spell it. It means 'fool' there. 'To hunt the gowk' means to go on a fool's errand. Happy hunting. G.

It was raining in New York, and the sky and buildings looked in on Hondorp sick with the pockmarks of the weather. The rain beat against his window as if inside his skin. He stretched his arms out on his desk and put his head down. 'A gok disguised,' he said out loud. 'A gok disguised,' his voice came back. His arm had released the dictaphone switch. Hondorp slammed his fist on the desk, and yelled, 'Let's cut out this shit.' The machine played it back, and

Hondorp gave it the back of his hand, and sent it flying against the wall. He went over to the window and regarded the liquefaction of the city till his own tension deliquesced as well.

III

One evening, just about two weeks before You're On Camera went off the air, Poppa Hondorp, while watching Person to Person, fell off his armchair. By the time his lipoma smashed against the rug he was dead. Coronary occlusion. Marie discovered him at breakfast time and called Hondorp who taxied up to Central Park after telephoning a crematorium.

Poppa Hondorp was burned to his ashes before sundown. Hondorp pled religious reasons for the rapidity although no prayers were said at the ceremony. Indeed, there was no ceremony. And no one—including Hondorp—was present but the men who carried in the body and carried out the ashes. After some thought, Hondorp composed the following notice and carried it down himself to the *Times* Building: 'Osip Ondhorp, aged thirty-two, died yesterday at his home, 643 Pleasant Avenue, Brooklyn. There are no survivors.' The *Times* did not print the notice, only the name Osip Ondhorp. And so Poppa Hondorp became one of the very few New Yorkers whose passing received no space at all in the great newspaper.

Two days later, Hendricks asked Hondorp if he'd had their weekly call from Poppa. 'He died last Friday,' said Hondorp.

After a long, interpreting pause, Hendricks looked up into her partner's face, and said, 'That's it. That's it.'

'A pity,' said Hondorp. The war had broken out; he was only surprised that there had been so long a peace.

'Golk's knives were rubber. He played to scare, not to kill. You're for real. A Capone.'

'You want root and stalk, but you won't wait for the flower,' said Hondorp, his eyes soft but full of the misery of the logic which drove him. 'Some play; some don't. If you play, you can take any side you want any time you want to. You can change courts, change your strokes, change your partners, change yourself. Because when you're playing, nothing counts, the game, your partners, your self. You don't exist. One-third of a century it took me to work that out. If you think the cocoon can stop the wings from breaking out of its sides, you don't understand anything. You don't care for anything. Go on and weep.'

She breathed as if air were new to her lungs, as if lungs were new in her body. 'You think it all follows naturally, that honesty drives you to your prey. I'll tell you boy that that's just it, that's why I'm getting off. I can cross myself up and not feel I've committed treason. I don't kneel down to what I was, nor to what I am. You finger yourself like a novena. But Holy Christ, you've outrun yourself. The motion going on in you now is sheer mechanics. Wings! The only move you make is to change your own oil. Somnambulist.'

'You learned nothing.'

'I learned this,' she said, walked the two feet which separated them, put her face into kissing position and said gently, 'You're dead. You're extinct. You can't ever come back. I'm packing.'

'Naturally,' said Hondorp. He was well rid of her: she had got off the train before her ticket lapsed.

IV

Though there were but two weeks left in their contracts, none of the inner circle remained. Hondorp realized that it was Hendricks who had advised them to get out. Fitch and Benson sent identical notes, excusing themselves for leaving before the actual end but pleading opportunities in West Coast television.

A month later, when the You're On Camera offices had been taken over by a programme called Name Your Risk, and the Sutton Place apartment sold to an assistant of Lurcher's—Hondorp was back in his father's apartment—he passed Fitch on Sixth Avenue. He started to ask 'What about the West Coast?' but the ship's head dipped into the crowd and Fitch was gone. As far as Hondorp could learn, neither he nor any other golks of the inner circle ever worked in television again. Two months after he had seen Fitch, Hondorp was certain that he saw Klebba at the wheel of a taxi going into the Vanderbilt Avenue entrance of Grand Central Station.

He himself was headed for Chicago. A radio station there was looking for a disc jockey, and Hondorp's response to the advertisement in *Radio News* had drawn a promising answer.

He never saw any of the other golks again, at least in person, though in a newsreel shot of a horse race at Long-champs, he had a brief clear view of Hendricks. She was attached to the arm of the most brutal-looking man Hondorp had ever seen, and his first reaction was the amazed thought that she had gone back to her husband. The thought nearly started one of the dizzy spells he occasionally suffered now, so he drove it out of mind. 'I've been seeing things again,' he told himself.

His schedule kept him quite busy. His hours were from midnight to six a.m.; then he ate a large breakfast, took a walk, and then slept until four or five in the afternoon. After dinner, he sometimes went to a movie or to one of the non-credit courses at the Downtown College of the University of Chicago. He found it hard to study though, or even to read, especially as the rest of his time was spent in keeping up with the popular songs. He worked six days a week. On Thursdays—his day off—he sometimes cruised the streets, pretending that he was scouting golks.

Golk himself, he saw once more. There was no question at all about this, although the circumstances were unlikely enough. It was in the summer of 1957. Hondorp was taking his two-week vacation in California, hoping to latch on to some television job. He took an occasional afternoon to go sightseeing, and one afternoon found him going through the Paramount lot on the regular studio tour. Only one movie was shooting, and the tour watched a scene being shot. A mob of people were crowding through the doors of a bank whose funds had been embezzled by the lovable old bank president. The set consisted of the great façade of the building which was fastened to girders by immense ropes looped high above the arc lights shining down on the crowd. Two or three scene-shifters were up in the ropes, holding them tight on the girders against the surge of the crowds. One of the shifters was Golk. There was no question about it. In the darkness above the mikes and cameras and lights, his great skull was lit, a cold, brooding moon above the scene. Even from the separating distance, Hondorp could see that he looked older, and fatter; but, as always, he fitted in. He belonged. His stubby legs were pushed against one of the girders, spreadeagled. His arms were stretched along two ropes. He functioned. Hondorp was just about to shout up at him, when, with a portion of that mysterious insight which always cowed the golks, he looked down, saw Hondorp, smiled, and waved his palm to the right, almost losing his grip on one of the ropes. Hondorp returned the salute, then turned around and walked out of the studio.

That night, although he had a week's vacation time left, he took the train back to Chicago, all trace of his ambition, all desire for change gone absolutely and for ever.